starstruck

CYN BALOG

starstruck

Delacorte Press

Text copyright © 2011 by Cyn Balog
Jacket art copyright © 2011 by Shutterstock

All rights reserved. Published in the United States by Delacorte Press, an imprint of Random House Children's Books, a division of Random House, Inc., New York.

Delacorte Press is a registered trademark and the colophon is a trademark of Random House, Inc.

Visit us on the Web! www.randomhouse.com/teens

Educators and librarians, for a variety of teaching tools, visit us at www.randomhouse.com/teachers

Library of Congress Cataloging-in-Publication Data
Balog, Cyn
Starstruck / Cyn Balog. — 1st ed.
p. cm.
Summary: On a barrier island off the coast of New Jersey, sixteen-year-old Dough is surprised when her long-distance boyfriend returns after four years and still finds her beautiful, despite her seventy-pound weight gain.
ISBN 978-0-385-73850-7 (hc) — ISBN 978-0-385-90734-7 (lib. bdg.) — ISBN 978-0-375-89494-7 (ebook)
[1. Love—Fiction. 2. Astrology—Fiction. 3. Supernatural—Fiction. 4. Overweight persons—Fiction. 5. New Jersey—Fiction.] I. Title.
PZ7.B2138St 2011
[Fic]—dc22
2010021636

The text of this book is set in 11-point Baskerville Book.

Book design by Marci Senders

Printed in the United States of America

10 9 8 7 6 5 4 3 2 1

First Edition

To Brian, my sweetie

ACKNOWLEDGMENTS

Sprinkle-covered donuts go out to my family, who puts up with my insanity. As always, to Mandy Hubbard, for her gentle but incisive critiques. To the crew at Random House, including the wonderful Stephanie Elliott and Krista Vitola. To my amazing agent, Jim McCarthy. To the children on Lydia Lane who invented Gone with the Wind. To the Park Bakery in Seaside Park, New Jersey, for giving me a sweet way to spend the summer. And lastly, most importantly, thank you to my beautiful, lovely fans, who are more than the icing on the cake. They are the flour and the sugar and the eggs. As the old bakery shop wisdom goes:

> *As you ramble on through life, brother,*
> *Whatever be your goal,*
> *Keep your eye on the donut*
> *And not upon the hole.*

HEY! How's everything back east?!?
Things are so WEIRD here. Grandma
Bertha put a prune under my bed to
give me GOOD KARMA!!??????? I
thought it was a cockroach and now
I have a BIG purple BLOTCH on the
bottom of my shoe.

School is EVEN WEIRDER, believe it
or not!!!! People are CRAZY. They
are all so FULL of themselves. I
miss hanging out with U. I will
NEVER EVER find another U.

I WISH I could be with U at Cellar
this year. DON'T let any of them
put U down!!!!!!!!! UR worth MORE
than ALL of them COMBINED!!!!!!!

GWEN, I wanted to ask you SO MANY
TIMES before I went away if you
would EVER consider me as your
boyfiend instead of your boy
fiend???? Write back soon.

LOVE,
Wish

1

FOR THE FIRST TIME in four years, I've lost my appetite.

I mean, how can I think of eating when I can't even breathe?

"Look at her," my little sister, Evie, sings. "She's lost in love."

Evie has obviously been listening to my mother's eighties tapes too much. Love is the last thing on my mind. The first thing is sheer terror. Second is hopelessness. Third is a desire to run away, far away, into the night, screaming like a banshee.

I stare at the screen of my computer. My hands shake on the keyboard. I can just make out a bit of my reflection: my cheeks look like two fat red balloons, glistening in the sunlight slashing through my bedroom window. Evie and my mom hover above me, peering over my shoulders at another daily email from Wish. Normally I'd never let them within a five-mile radius of one of our top secret lovefests, but the five-alarm wail that escaped from my mouth must have made them think I'd just read that the island of Cellar Bay was sinking into the ocean.

At this point, that would be happy news.

MOM got a condo in Cellarton! Guess she couldn't STAND to be on the same island as MY DAD, ha ha! It's right by the bridge to Cellar Bay, though.

"Why didn't you tell us Wish is coming back here?" my mom asks, kneading my shoulder like I'm one of her famous breads.

If I had known, she would have, too. It would have been obvious. I would have sworn off white cream donuts and Tae-Boed myself into a stupor. Squirreled away some of my earnings from the bakery to buy a hot new wardrobe, and invested the rest in that miracle acne cure celebrities are always peddling on infomercials. Now there's no time. I'd need a year to get back to my twelve-year-old self. And a fairy godmother. Instead, my long-distance boyfriend, Philip P. Wishman III, will be on a collision course with planet Gwendolyn, all 234 pounds of her, in, oh, t minus seventy-six hours.

My mom studies the email. "Does it say why he's coming back?"

I shrug, numb. Because he wants to prove to me that just when you think your life is at its absolute suckiest, it can always get worse?

"We'll have him over for dinner," she says, completely oblivious to my meltdown.

"Ma, you want to welcome him, not kill him," Evie points out.

Though my mom knows everything about baking, that's where her knowledge of food ends. My mom's fanciest dinners are really prepared by Mrs. Paul or the Gorton's fisherman. But her culinary skills, or lack thereof, are the least of my concerns. I read the last line again:

I can't wait to see you IN PERSON finally and KISS my BEAUTIFUL GIRLFRIEND. It's been like a DREAM for me for SO LONG!!!

Wish has a knack for unnecessarily capitalizing everything and overusing exclamation points, like a ten-year-old girl, which is something I never realized until we started emailing back and forth each day. At first, I didn't mind it, but now it annoys me. Of course, maybe I wouldn't be annoyed if I wasn't so sure his enthusiasm was going to totally deflate within seconds of seeing me. He doesn't know I'm not worthy of three exclamation points. I'm probably not even worthy of a measly comma. The only recent pictures I've sent him were from the neck up, or so fuzzed out that I looked like the Blob in drag. But none of this is my fault. It's his fault for deciding to let his mother take him across the country to L.A. to live with his wacko grandmother when his parents split up. It's his fault for leaving me so heartbroken and alone that the first thing I did after watching his mother's BMW pull away was sit in the back room of the bakery and eat an entire tray of cannoli. His fault for sending me a daily email for the past four years, making me salivate so much for a kiss from him that all I could do to tell my mouth to behave was fill it with jelly donuts. *His fault.*

5

"He can't come back here," I say, digging my fingernails into the skin of my fleshy thighs, which somehow seem even bigger than they did when I woke up this morning. "Our relationship is perfect the way it is."

Evie snorts. "You're so weird, Dough."

I bury my face in my hands. That's another thing. I have no social life. No friends. Nothing normal, non-weird people have. Nothing, except him.

And twenty bucks says soon I won't even have that.

2

FIRST LET ME EXPLAIN something about the kissing, or lack thereof. Wish and I have been best friends ever since first grade, when we fought over Curious George at Cellar Bay Elementary School, this little brick building on Main where we were two of a handful of students. But a love for that cheeky monkey wasn't the only thing we had in common, we realized. Soon we were the complete-each-other's-sentences kind of friends. We were always together, like peanut butter and jelly.

We stayed best friends until right before junior high, when he moved away. That was when his parents split up and his mom took him to live with her mother, Grandma Bertha, this real nutcase of a woman who always used to talk about auras and astrology and that kind of crap. The one time she visited Jersey, she told me that my aura was black and dead and that I was invading her peace, which was just fine with me, because she was obviously insane. I felt bad that a normal guy like Wish had to live with such a creepy old lady.

So anyway, our relationship didn't develop into a boyfriend-girlfriend thing until he'd been in California for a while. After we'd emailed back and forth for two months, he asked me out. In real life, Wish is a total wuss when it comes to his feelings, like most guys, but he turned out to be a lot more confident in email. I could tell he was lonely at his new swanky private school in L.A., because he kept saying how much he missed me and how he would never find another girl like me. I'm sure it didn't help that Grandma Bertha kept putting things like dead moths and dried prunes under his pillow at night to "clear away the evil spirits."

And it wasn't much better for me; there was no junior high on the island of Cellar Bay, so I was suddenly thrust into a big school on the mainland, Cellarton Junior High, where everybody knew each other and nobody knew me. Though he was three thousand miles away, even Wish knew all the students better than I did, because his family had been in some exclusive country club with them. They were all rich, and, well, I come from a coupon-clipping, water-down-the-ketchup-to-make-it-last-longer kind of family. They respected him, and they still do, because his Facebook page is filled with a slew of "What's up on the West Coast, W?" comments daily from classmates who don't even know I exist. If Wish had been with me, I think I would have been accepted, because they would have accepted him. But as it was, I was an outcast the day I stepped off the island, into their world.

Luckily, Wish's emails always cheered me up. "Don't let them put you down," he'd say, followed by fourteen exclamation points. "You're worth more than all of them combined." Then he wrote—and I remember it like it was yesterday—"Gwen," using my real name instead of my nickname, so I knew it was serious, "I wanted to ask you so many times before I went away if you would ever consider me as your boyfriend instead of your boy friend." But he misspelled "friend" as "fiend" and for some reason I found that so funny that I snorted Pepsi out my nose. I wrote back some stupid flowery thing about how I would love for him to be my fiend, and it was on.

Still, for four years, our romance has only consisted of email, IMs, and the occasional phone call. He writes on my wall a lot, too; I wouldn't even be on Facebook if it weren't for him, because he is the only one who does. But no kisses. No hugs. Not even hand-holding, and yes, I realize that makes us the most pathetic couple in North America.

But it can only get worse when he sees me in the flesh. He goes on and on about his baseball games, the wild parties, and all the other things happening in his life, so much so that L.A. seems like a completely different, sexier world. He sends me pictures, too, of himself and his friends, and they all look like they could be on their own prime-time television show on the CW. I'm sure there was a progression, but when I look back, it seems like almost overnight he went from gangly, goofy, and whining about how conceited and self-absorbed everyone was, to tan, easy on the eyes, and just plain nothing like me. I knew that he was in danger of lapsing into a coma while reading my amazing news, which usually consisted of whatever new donut flavor we were rolling out that week. I'd thought about lying, making up stories about how I was traveling to the Amazon or auditioning for *America's Next Top Model*. I'd come pretty close to it a few times—not auditioning; I'm not out of my mind. Lying.

Now I'm really, really glad I didn't.

I'm standing behind the counter, right over a tray of freshly baked elephant ears, not even sure how I got here or how I managed to make it through the morning without losing a finger or two in the bread slicer. I push a white paper bag across the counter to a prune-faced old lady and say, "That'll be fifty-eight. Um, dollars."

Her eyes get even more squinty. "For three donuts?"

Hmm, come to think of it, even though Reilly's Irish Bakery is the only place to get food on the island besides the 7-E, we don't price-gouge that much. Fifty-eight is, at last count, the number of hours separating me from a reunion that could only be made more painful if I decided to sit on him. I do the calculation again. "Three twenty. Um, three dollars and twenty cents," I say lightly, thumping the side of my head as if to say, "What was I thinking?"

She reaches into one of those tiny needlepoint change purses that it seems like all the rich ladies on the island walk around with, though they probably only hold one-zillionth of their net worth, and pulls out a few wrinkled dollars and two dimes. "That's a little better," she snaps, giving me a severe "I'm keeping my eye on you" glare.

10

Someone taps me on the shoulder. I jump almost high enough to take out the ceiling fan above, then spin around and nearly whack Evie in her newly sprouted rack, which, incidentally, is already bigger than mine, though I outweigh her by over one hundred pounds. Where's the justice in that? "What?" I growl, turning to the manual cash register and stuffing the money inside.

She rolls her eyes and inspects her manicure. "Dough, you are so weird."

"Shouldn't you be upstairs, sleeping?"

She rolls her eyes again. "No, you should be. It's ten after one."

I look at the clock on the wall over the freezer case. It is. Never has my shift at the bakery gone so quickly. I wonder if I can go upstairs and lipo my thighs with a vacuum, or if that would leave a scar.

Evie looks bright and cheerful and beautiful, as usual. Talking about justice—between Evie and me, there is none. I was the firstborn, and my father, when he was still in the picture, insisted that I be named after his great-grandmother Gwendolyn, who had a mustache and whose name, ironically, could be shortened to Dough. According to my mother, he insisted on a lot of things, which is why they never got along. Then, two years later, my mother inherited the bakery from her parents and decided to leave my father even though she was six months pregnant. She liked the name Evan—a name that would work for a boy or a girl—because a supermodel of the time had it. Maybe it was prophetic, because thirteen years later, Evie began to look like a fashion model, and I started to resemble the Pillsbury Doughboy.

11

Another injustice is that at sixteen, as the eldest and "most responsible," I'm stuck with the crazy morning shift, and Evie gets the leisurely afternoon shift. I have to wake up at three-thirty, trudge downstairs, and help the baker, Hans, then help my mom load the trays, stock the shelves, and get all prepared so that we're ready to go when the store opens at five and the throngs of wealthy Cellar Bay residents come to get their breakfast. Then, after the store is nearly sold out and the crowds have gone, I trudge upstairs, looking like the undead, and take a nap while Evie begins her shift, which involves sitting in the back room and reading *Glamour* while she waits for her one customer of the afternoon to arrive.

But enough about Princess Evie. I'm just starting to untie my apron strings, which Evie can thread around her waist three times and tie in the front but I can barely get behind me, when the bell on the door jingles and in walks my worst nightmare. Actually, three of them.

It's Rick Rothman, king of the egos, and two of his buddies, Narcissistic and Big Head. They're barefoot, but unfortunately, we allow that, because we're a beach establishment. Otherwise I would love an excuse to kick them out. They have on Oakley blades and wet suits unzipped down the front to bare their bronzed chests. I know they've left their longboards out on the front walk for old ladies to trip over, like they usually do. I grunt and try to escape into the back room, but not before I hear Rick's nasally voice:

"Look, guys, it's the number ten."

Narc and B.H. guffaw like gorillas, which is the required practice of a Rothman Disciple. I half expect them to start beating their chests. Evie just sits there, looking embarrassed for me. She's never been queen of the comeback; fortunately, though, after four years of school with these guys, I've had a lot of practice. Like I've never heard people refer to me and my skinny sister standing next to me as the number ten. Totally unoriginal, but Rick doesn't need originality to have the zombies of Cellarton High hang on his every word. I stop untying my apron and saunter up to the cabinet. "Look, Evie, it's the number zero."

He acts like he didn't hear me, then props his elbows up on the counter, as if he's deciding what he wants to order. Which is totally stupid, since he's been coming here with his boys for years and always orders the same thing.

Evie clears her throat. "Can I get you guys something?"

He eyes my sister. "Yeah, baby. You can get me to understand how the same parents produced this tub of lard"—he points to me, then points to her—"and such a beautiful creature as you."

I guess if Evie had not just come into that incredible rack and transformed from Awkward Gangly Evie into Showstopping Gorgeous Evie over the summer, she might have realized that Rick, for all his good looks, is the biggest player on the Eastern Seaboard. She might have seen through his act. Poor Nai-Evie. She melts into a puddle right before our eyes. I can't blame her; Rick is easily the hottest guy in the school. And the biggest jerk, too, but when he aims those giant blue eyes in your direction, it's hard to see that. Not that it's ever happened to me, but I've heard enough talk in the girls' locker room to know that he has taken dozens of victims.

"Excuse me while I vomit," I mutter.

He ignores me. "You coming to Cellarton High this year?"

She nods and squeaks out, "I'll be a freshman."

"Fantastic. I'll keep an eye out for you."

I head into the back room and get a bag, consider puking in it, then fill it up with two white creams, one Boston cream, and a sugar ring. When I come back into the front, Rick is leaning so far over the counter toward Evie that he could quite possibly stick his tongue in her ear if he so chose. She's blushing, which on me looks like I have hives, but on her looks irresistible.

"Your order," I say, holding the bag up to him to break up the lovefest. "With the chocolate milk it comes to five, even."

He turns to look at me, a question on his face.

"You guys get the same thing every time you come in here," I explain.

He reaches into the pocket of his wet suit and pulls out the money. "Thanks, Dough."

He doesn't seem quite so mean now. It almost makes me feel bad for smearing his donuts on the floor in the back room before placing them in the bag.

Almost.

I HEAD UPSTAIRS, stuffing another donut in my mouth, which does wonders in stopping the flow of tears. Girls are supposed to look up to their big sisters, but I think Evie is embarrassed by me now. It started when she entered sixth grade and I was in eighth, and she saw how everyone treated me. Before then, she used to follow me around and try to borrow my clothes and lip gloss and sleep in my bed. But then, that very first day, the second we stepped off the bus at Cellarton Junior High and someone called me lard-ass, the big-sister worship was over.

If Wish had been here, I tell myself, things would have been different. Even though he and Rick travel in the same wealthy-beyond-my-wildest-imagination circles, Rick always rubbed him the wrong way. He could have told Rick where to go or beaten him up, defended my honor, just like in the movies. And then we would have laughed together and poked fun at how nobody else could fit in a room with Rick and his ego.

Oh, who am I kidding? Rick isn't the only one who makes jokes about me. No one wants a girlfriend who's the butt of 99 percent of the school's jokes. (The rest are about the purple chicken the cafeteria passes off on Thursdays.)

My family lives in a three-bedroom apartment above the bakery. It's old, probably the oldest building around. It's the only establishment on the island, besides the 7-E, the elementary school, and a gas station down the road, that isn't a multimillion-dollar mansion. The owners call them cottages, because that sounds quaint, but they're bigger than shopping malls. I've heard that it's bad luck not to name a ship, and I guess that also applies to houses that touch the ocean, because they all have goofy names like the Whitecap or Sea Spray. Wish's dad, a retired naval officer turned author of bestselling thrillers, has one of the biggest; there's a sign outside, rimmed in rope, with an anchor on it, that reads Red Sky at Night. Rick Rothman's parents, who are both scum-sucking (well, I just assume they're scum-suckers, since he's already one) lawyers, have one that's pink and horrendous, like Miami Beach came here for the day and threw up on it. It's called Seashell Cove. Supposedly, their winter house, ten miles inland, has turrets and a moat and would make King Arthur drool. I think they also have houses in other places, for other seasons, too. The Rothmans are fortunate enough to be able to change houses like they change the batteries in their smoke alarms.

But I live in the little apartment over the bakery. If we

had to name our home, I could just see the sign, hanging over the cracked sidewalk, with fancy script: The Slum. The kitchen is part of the living room, and the only things that separate the bedrooms from the living area are plastic shower curtains. Plus the floor kind of tilts, pretty badly, toward the left front corner of the building, where my room is. Drop a marble on the linoleum, and eventually, I'll end up sleeping with it.

Even though we're within walking distance of those mansions, it feels like a million miles away. Cellar Bay is one of the barrier islands off the coast of New Jersey; it's just a tiny strip, a half mile wide, tied to Cellarton, on the mainland, by a rickety two-lane drawbridge. It gets pretty busy in the summer, when all the residents over the bridge flood the beach. I guess I should be grateful for that, because it's what keeps the bakery in business, but having to cater to the Ricks of the world during my summer vacation is more than one poor soul should have to bear.

My mom is working in her office, which is our wobbly three-legged kitchen table. Usually once a week, she pulls out all the bills and her ledger (my mother refuses to keep anything on a computer), and her grunts and groans and cries of frustration can be heard all over the island. She breaks a pencil in her hands and blows out air so that the thick tuft of red hair over her eyes puffs out. "They raised the price of apple-raspberry jelly again. Again!" Her face distorts and she clenches her fists and I think maybe an alien might pop out of her belly.

"Bad news," I say, even though I can't muster the same amount of outrage. "We can put less in the donuts."

She glares at me, and I know what she's going to say. "Four generations of Reillys have stuck to these recipes. I don't intend to change them. But . . ." She looks down at the pile of bills. "I wish I knew why I'm always coming up short. We're barely scraping by."

This reminds me of a Far Side cartoon someone taped to my locker once, of a bakery manager saying, "I don't understand it; we're just scraping by!" while there's this guy sweeping up who is the size of a Mack truck. Okay, I do eat a lot, but so does Evie. She may be skinny, but she's a walking trash can, our vastly different metabolisms being yet another sore spot for me. Still, I'd be the first one blamed for the failure of the bakery.

The thought makes me so upset that I head into my bedroom without another word. There, I pull off my whites, which are all gritty and smell of cinnamon sugar, and stare at myself in the mirror. Yeah, there's no question I could stand to lose a few dozen pounds. I look like a turkey, with a big fat stomach, a beak nose, and a pouch of skin hanging down from my chin. A turkey with frizzy, mousy brown hair. And my cheeks are full and perpetually red, like two giant pimples on the verge of popping.

Oh, but I'm not all weird. My mother once told me that all people in the world have some God-given gift, something special about them. I have nice toes. Nice feet in general. I could be a foot model.

I know, la-di-da. I guess there are worse gifts that a person could have, but I know for sure there are better ones.

Wish, on the other hand, is the most gifted person I know. Not only can he read the ingredients on the back of a cereal box and make them sound interesting, but he is an amazing artist. He can draw anything; just give him a pencil. Usually, he draws planets and rocket ships; he's always been fascinated by astronomy. My eyes trail to the bulletin board over my desk, where there's a drawing of my profile, with stars and planets in orbit around my head, on a bakery box top. He did it in seconds while I was on the phone, taking down a birthday cake order as we were sitting in the back of the bakery playing Monopoly. I look pretty in that picture. Maybe I was, back then.

I don't have a closet in my room, so my mother has hung some of my new school clothes from a garment rack in the corner. She's freshly pressed them, but they're still terrible, styleless, fat-girl pants and shirts from Wal-Mart. Things that people wear when they don't care how they look. I didn't mind them last week, when she brought them home, but now . . .

"Mom, can we go to the mainland?" I ask after changing into my gym shorts and T-shirt.

When I pull back the shower curtain, Mom's staring at me like I have three heads. I never want to go anywhere; all my favorite activities, TV watching and sleeping, can be done in the luxury of my bedroom. "Why?"

"To get some school clothes. And to get my hair cut?" There's a pretty nice mall a few minutes inland that all my classmates go to, but if I can get there in the next hour or so, while they're all at the beach, I'll probably avoid them. I've heard some of the girls talk about this cool hair salon, Swank, which is right in the mall. There's a small chance that nice hair and clothes might so completely mesmerize

Wish that he'll overlook my extra pounds. Well, that and some hallucinogenic drugs, which I've heard can also be bought on the mainland.

She gives me a look. "Seriously, Gwen, did I not just finish telling you how we're barely scraping by?"

I stare blankly. Oh, right. I do seem to recall her saying something about that.

"What's wrong with the clothes I just bought you?"

"Well," I say. Where do I start? "They're fat-girl clothes."

"No, they're perfectly useful and comfortable pants and shirts. The styles are a smart choice for people of any size," she says. This from a woman whose best ensemble includes a free Grand Opening T-shirt from an electronics store that went out of business five years ago.

"But . . ."

"Aw, hon, I know you want to look good for Wish," she says, reading my mind. She picks through her purse, and I think for a second that she's going to go for it. Instead, she pulls out a ten, places it on the kitchen table, and says, "Here. Go to Melinda's and get a good shaping."

Oh, no. Melinda is like eighty years old. She's our neighbor who runs the hotel next door and, wackily, in her spare time, cuts hair. She comes from a time when there were only three people in a village, so the postman was also the veterinarian and the editor of the town paper. Unfortunately, I don't think she was sent to Paris to study the latest styling techniques, like the girls at Swank were. Last time I let her have her way with my hair, she gave me a Farrah Fawcett feather. And there is nothing worse than a fat girl pretending to be one of the original Charlie's Angels.

I finally decide that my hair, which is frizzy and out of control, couldn't look any worse, no matter how badly or reminiscent of a seventies TV star she cuts it. I pocket the money and head out the door, thinking that if this is my only option for improvement before Wish gets here, I might as well make that lipo date with the vacuum cleaner.

4

"DID YOU KNOW that L.A. has the thinnest population in the country?" Melinda says as she sits me in her old-fashioned barbershop chair, which is, oddly, in the lobby of the hotel. There's crocheted stuff everywhere, products of another one of Melinda's hobbies; I think the Seascape Hotel is where doilies go on vacation. An old guy in Bermuda shorts and knee-high black dress socks, with zinc oxide slathered all over his nose, comes by for the free hot tea and finger sandwiches that Melinda serves every day at two. He grabs two big handfuls of dainty cucumber sandwiches and then sits in one of the chairs, chewing with his mouth open and staring at me as if I'm the afternoon entertainment.

"No," I say, wondering if she can just stab me in the throat with her scissors and get it over with.

"Plastic surgery, my dear," she says, tilting my chin up so that I can see my face in the mirror. "You have a natural beauty."

I stare at my face. I have nice, big blue eyes. It really isn't that bad when you look at me head-on and can't see the beak of my nose. That, and if I didn't have a body attached, I would be fine. If I could just be a floating head that never turned sideways, people would love me, I am sure, providing that Melinda doesn't Farrah me up.

"Now, what do we want to do here?" she asks, fluffing my frizzy hair over my shoulders.

Melinda is so senile that two minutes later she won't remember what I say, so I decide to be short and to the point. And I decide I will repeat the directions every so often, in case she forgets. "Keep it as long as possible. But put in bangs. And long layers."

She nods and gets to work. I'm a little nervous, with the way she's clipping so frantically, that I'm in trouble. "You know," she says, peeking over her bifocals at my reflection, "my daughter is your size, and I keep telling your mother to come and take some of the clothes she left here. Why don't you try some of them on, at least?"

I don't have the heart to tell Melinda that her daughter, who stayed with her for a year while she and her husband were "working things out," is a prostitute. It was obvious to all except Melinda, who called her Doll Baby, that wherever she'd come from, she must have spent many hours on a street corner there. Everyone in the neighborhood knew it. Evie said she saw tracks on her arms, but then again, Evie watches too much *CSI*, so I can't take her seriously. But anyway, is it possible to wear a snakeskin minidress and not be a streetwalker?

"Um, I just got a bunch of new clothes," I say. "But thanks."

"Oh, okay. But I don't think she's ever coming back. She's a bit of a gypsy, that one. And she never calls or writes. I haven't seen her in almost a year," Melinda babbles, and I notice she's looking at the plate of finger sandwiches across the way, maybe trying to determine if there are enough, or maybe she's just trying to figure out if there is any surface left in the lobby that could use another doily. Meanwhile, she snips off what seems like a pretty long lock of hair.

"Remember, long as possible, long layers," I repeat. "Bangs."

"Oh, I know, dear!" she sings. "I know all about glamour. I cut Lena Horne's hair. She stayed here once."

I have no idea who that is. I just hope she doesn't have a mullet.

Twenty minutes later, I walk out of Melinda's hotel with a plate of finger sandwiches, a bag of prostitute clothes, and a weird wedge on my head that makes me look like you could tip me upside down and fill it with cream of mushroom soup.

I need another donut.

5

THAT NIGHT, I get an email from Wish:

Hey, G,
All the flights out of LA were
booked solid for Labor Day weekend,
so my mom booked me on a flight for
Tuesday. I am so BUMMED I am going
to MISS the FIRST DAY OF SCHOOL!!!
Take good NOTES for me, k?
What is up with you? Still
counting down the MINUTES till you
see me? HA HA. You sounded a
little weird in your LAST email.
Is everything ALL RIGHT?
W.

That is the best news ever. Another day. One more day of the possibility that a truck might run me over.

I'm sure Wish must be catching my drift that I'm not exactly bubbling with excitement to see him. My reply to him was less than cordial, as if he'd murdered my family and I'd just found out he'd been let out of prison, something like "WHY? Are you sure?" Then I told him that L.A. had the thinnest and most beautiful population in the country, as if that would make him change his mind. I knew that if I wanted to give him a real deal-breaker, it would be easy; all I would have to do was send him a photocopy of my butt. But I love Wish. I don't want to break off our relationship; I just want him to never find out that his girlfriend is a whale. What's so wrong with that?

My mother is making dinner—fish sticks or fish filets or pieces of fish in fish-shaped patties—and the smell is so thick my mouth starts to water. Yes, Stomach wants me to eat again, even though Brain is shouting, No, no, never ever. I decide that maybe I could be one of those sick souls who control their appetites with exercise. They say it becomes a habit after a week, so after seven days, I'll be my new health-minded self, and Wish will be so awed by my dedication to fitness that he'll totally forget about the junk in my trunk.

I tear my eyes away from the mirror and the train wreck that is my haircut, and pull out my Tae Bo video. Then I get to work. Billy's been screaming at me for a full thirty minutes and I'm about to be washed away in the tide of my own sweat when Evie pokes her head through the shower curtain. She's nibbling on one of Melinda's finger sandwiches.

Her shift must be over. "Oh, God, I thought you were moving pianos up here."

I don't bother to look at her. Huff out, "Piano. My ass. What's the difference?"

"Don't let what those guys said to you . . ." She begins another one of her halfhearted, I've-always-been-thin-so-I-have-no-idea-what-it's-like pep talks, but then stops. Over a particularly tough back-kick that has me nearly dislocating my butt, if that's even possible, I see her face, frozen in horror. "What the hell happened to your hair?"

"Nothing."

She comes closer, inspecting it. Then she reaches out and pats the top of it. "It looks like a triangle or something. Like Cleopatra's pyramid is sitting on your head."

"I'm trying to start a new trend," I pant. "Hair shaped like the Seven Wonders of the World. I think the Hanging Gardens of Babylon would really bring out the color in your eyes."

Billy now has us—me and all the way overexcited people in his cult—doing "ricochet kicks" on one leg, which I manage to do for half a second before I lose my balance and fall against a wall. The entire building shakes.

"What was that?" my mom calls.

"Earthquake," I mumble from the puddle of sweat I've collapsed into in the center of my room. "Run for cover. Save yourself."

Evie is still looking at the atrocity over my eyes. She keeps her hair long, like this platinum waterfall, so even if a seagull came and pooped on her head, it would work for her. "Good luck with that."

I roll over and look at her. "That guy—Rick. He's a total tool. You'll want to stay away from him."

She nods in agreement. "Oh, totally. What a jerk."

Ten bucks says she didn't even hear me and is wondering which of her Barbie-sized outfits would be best to make him drool on the first day of school. Something with a bare midriff, I bet. Evie likes to show off her belly button. I probably would, too, if I had such a cute one and not something big and foreboding that looks like the mouth of hell.

Afterward, at dinner, to keep my mind off the delectable array of epicurean delights (har-har) before me, I read the entertainment section of the newspaper. It seems that all the September television premieres feature teen characters who are thinner than waxed paper. The obligatory "fat best friend" is probably no bigger than a size six. I have half a stick of fish and some frozen green beans. I try to tell myself that I'm full, despite Stomach's telling everyone at the table otherwise.

"What's wrong?" my mother asks, reaching over to feel my forehead, which is still sticky with sweat from my date with Billy. "You sick?"

Evie grins and bats her eyelashes. "Lovesick! She's thinking about Wish."

I think about poking her with my fork, but since she's so skinny, I'd probably pierce a major organ.

"Your hair looks great. Melinda did a fantastic job," my mother, who I never realized was blind until this moment, says. She, however, has spent most of her life in a hair-net, and it doesn't even faze her to run errands, go shopping, even meet with friends wearing it.

"Ma. I have a point on my forehead. I can impale people on it."

She eyes it critically. "Wash it out. It might surprise you."

Evie nods.

"If I don't accidentally slit my wrists when I reach up to touch it," I mutter, holding a green bean between my fingers and squeezing it. "That would be a surprise."

My mother waves me away. "So does Wish need us to pick him up from Philly on Monday?"

I shake my head. "He couldn't get a flight. He's coming in Tuesday."

"Oh. Well, that's good. I need you at the bakery to train the winter help," she says, to my delight. I just love training new employees on the last weekend of summer vacation. "He's missing the first day of school?"

I shrug. "Guess so."

"Well, that's a bummer."

I'm thinking it's not. The jokes are always worst the first day of school. That's when everyone is really giving each other the once-over, to see the tans, the new clothes, the monumental fatness, whatever. Maybe I can get all the teasing over with on Tuesday so that when Wish comes in, he won't hear any of it.

Of course, he's not an idiot. You don't have to be on the honor roll to notice that nobody writes on my Facebook wall, and when they do, it's usually some unkind remark about my butt that I have to scramble to delete. But people were making fun of me long before I packed on the pounds. I can't help flashing back to one summer night, when I was surrounded by crystal chandeliers, brass fixtures shinier than the sun, and horribly gaudy velvet flowered wallpaper. The restroom of Cellarton Country Club. It was the club's summer banquet, four years ago, right before Wish moved away. He'd invited me because his parents were dragging him and he hated those things, and for once they'd said he could bring a guest. Maybe they felt guilty about the impending divorce or thought that having an outsider there would help keep things civil.

It was a mistake from the beginning. First the car on the ride over was as deathly quiet as the bakery on a winter afternoon. Then, about an hour into it, while Wish was getting me a drink, I felt like everyone was staring at me, so I decided to go to the ladies' room. While I was in the restroom, doing my business, a gaggle of giggling girls came in to reapply their lip gloss or whatever gaggles of girls do when they go to the bathroom together. I remember that I didn't have any nice shoes, so I had to wear these embarrassing, scuffed-up sandals that were closer to brown than the original white. I'm not really sure who the girls were, but I heard them whisper the word "trash" and it sounded like someone was moving furniture outside my stall. The next thing I knew, they left and turned the lights out. And there I was, in this unfamiliar, pitch-black bathroom with my panties around my knees. I quickly stood up and fumbled for the latch, but when I unlocked it, the door would not budge. Something was on the other side. I tried to get out, but I was stuck. At first I prayed that someone other than Wish, someone I didn't know, would come for me, because it was so embarrassing. As the minutes wore on, though, I started praying that anyone would save me. Eventually, Wish did. He heard me screaming and braved the ladies' restroom for me. The most horrible thing was that when he opened the door, most of my dress was tucked into my pink panties with the word "peace" on them. I still cringe whenever I think of that, of Wish seeing me that way. But he didn't laugh or anything; he just told his mom I needed to leave and they took me straight home. I can still remember him apologizing over and over again. "I'm sorry, so sorry, Dough. They're not usually like that." And I thought, Okay, maybe they're not. When I started at Cellarton Junior High, I was fully prepared to give them another chance.

But the truth was they *were* usually like that. To me, at least.

My mother shakes the table a little. The ice in my glass of Diet Coke clinks and some of it spills onto the plastic checked tablecloth, nudging me from the memory. "Don't get down. It's just one more day," she says.

I reach across the table and sigh, "And this is just one more fish stick," and practically swallow the whole thing without chewing.

6

EVIE HAS BEEN AT BAND CAMP all weekend. A lot of people
think band camp is lame, but she's on the band front, which
is the small subset of band that is right up there with the
cheerleaders. That's probably because they wear skintight
leotards with butt-cheek-baring skirts, which makes them
just about everything the football players are looking for in
their girlfriends. Granted, Evie has talent. She twirls a baton
and has been able to do so since she was six. The first time
I picked one up, I knocked myself unconscious. But Evie is
a natural. And she loves twirling so much that this morning, Labor Day, the final day of camp, she jazz-kicked her
way into the store for a carton of OJ and a couple of donuts,
even though it was only six. She was wearing short shorts
and a T-shirt and had a bag slung over her shoulder and
was shivering in excitement (or perhaps because it was a bit

nippy and her shorts went all the way up her butt crack) as she waited for her best friend Becca's mom to pick her up. She even practiced some tosses and moves she learned at cheerleading camp this summer, just to make sure she "still had it" or something. The old ladies in the store smiled at her, then growled at me for not getting their Danishes fast enough.

It's ironic that it's Labor Day, because what have I been doing for my last day of freedom before my junior year? Working. Working like crazy. Because of Evie's extracurriculars, I've been picking up the slack at the bakery the entire weekend. I know there are child labor laws that prevent this, but there must be a loophole in there that says if the child belongs to you—i.e., you pushed said child out your hoohah—you may disregard any regulations designed to prevent said child from collapsing in exhaustion.

Here it is, the day before school starts, and I look like a zombie. A zombie who has eaten half the junior class, but a zombie nonetheless. Yeah, Billy totally let me down. I've been working out with him and his cult every night for an hour, and I've gained three pounds! And with my triangle hair, I'm sure to make everyone jealous tomorrow.

When Wish sees me, that will really make my life complete.

My mother comes in from the back, looking seriously put out. She has her hands on her hips and there's flour dotted in her hair. "They're not here yet?"

I shrug. "Who?"

She looks at me, clearly disappointed that I don't breathe this business the way she does. "The winter help."

I check the clock. It's one exactly. "What time were they supposed to be here?"

She puckers her lips. "One."

"It's one right now."

"So. If they walk through the door right now, or any-time later, that means they're officially late. And what kind of example does that set, if they can't even show up on time on the first day of work?"

Knowing the type of people my mom has gotten to be the winter help for the past few years, I think the woman probably got her walker stuck in a crack on the sidewalk or lost her direction because of Alzheimer's. We have to get new help year after year, because our winter help always dies from old age over the summer. It's not my mom's fault; those are the only people around during the winter, because this island becomes a graveyard. All the rich people with kids usually move to their winter homes on the mainland, so I end up taking the short bus to school.

The bell on the door jingles. Standing in the doorframe, his head directly in front of the Fresh Baked Bread! sign, is a kid with so many tattoos on his arms I can't even be sure he has skin. He's darting his chin back and forth as if watching a tennis match, and he looks a little lost, not like he wants a cruller. His hands are clenched over a paper bag, and he's wearing army fatigue pants and a rumpled, sleeve-less tie-dyed shirt. I turn to my mom and mouth, "Is that him?"

She gives me a worried look and nods.

"He, um, looks like an escaped convict," I whisper.

She tightens her lips and says, "They promised me he

34

didn't do anything bad," and before I can ask her who she meant by "they," and what she meant by "bad," she's giving him her famous fake smile. "Chris?"

Oh, no. My mom hired a criminal. She must have killed off all the old people on the island, and this was her only option.

He nods and gives a slow, easy smile, one that means he either wants to rip her head off or buy a puppy. I can't tell which, because his eyes are completely covered by a mass of black pseudodreads. "Christian," he mutters.

She turns businesslike. "I'm Tammy Reilly. This is my daughter Gwen. She'll give you a feel for your duties."

I expect him to get hung up on the space below my boobs, where all my fat is, but he doesn't. He just gives an almost imperceptible nod and looks around the room. He even inspects the far corners of the ceiling, maybe looking for pink elephants or whatever, and that's when his hair flips back and I get a look at his eyes. They're bleary. I think he's high, but I don't bring this to my mother's attention, because I can't speak.

My mother is going to make me work with a criminal.

"So," I hear her say, "if you need anything, just call. I'll be upstairs working on the ledger."

Correction: My mother is going to make me work with a criminal *alone*.

By the time my vocal cords start to thaw, I hear the screen door out back close and my mom's feet shuffle up the rickety staircase to our apartment.

She's left me alone with a criminal.

I take a step backward and clap my hands together to

keep them from shaking. "So!" I say, as if I have some idea what to follow that with.

I don't.

He stands there for a long, uncomfortable moment. Then he holds out his paper bag and shrugs, as if to say, "What should I do with this?"

"Um, yeah, you can put that back here," I say, motioning into the back room. "And I should get you an apron."

Though I've walked through the door to the back room—where we keep trays of extra food to restock the shelves, boxes and bags and supplies, and the lockers for employees—a million times, I somehow end up tripping over my feet. I figure one of my no-name Keds knock-offs must be untied, but no, they're both fine. I am just an idiot.

I open a locker for him and then pull a clean apron from the stack. I usually feel all sweaty when I meet people. Maybe it's because I'm usually all sweaty. It's one of the reasons I don't go to the beach, and it's why antiperspirant is my best friend. But now the sweat is cascading off my forehead like Niagara Falls.

"Um, I guess I'll show you how to use the cash register first," I say, wondering if that's a good idea. He can just knock me over, steal the money, and be gone. Well, maybe not knock me over, but the rest would be pretty easy, since I'm not sure I can use my Tae Bo moves for real-life situations. However, since I just cleaned out the register and there's probably no more than fifty dollars in it, I figure it's no major sacrifice.

I give him the rundown, something I've done with all

our employees. He doesn't ask a thousand stupid questions, not like the old ladies I'm used to training. He just nods, and when I ask, "Got it?" he gives me a smile. Not a nice, cheery one, though. That would have put me at ease. This one is decidedly Joker-like. Creepy.

As I'm explaining our pricing for cookies and how to use the scale to weigh them, I realize he's not paying attention. He's looking out the window. I follow his line of vision, expecting to see a girl in a bikini or something, but I see nothing. There's a house across the street that's being gutted, and a huge Dumpster outside, filled with broken glass glinting in the sunlight, but that's about it. I raise my voice. "And a full pound will fit in one of these boxes. Okay?"

His nod is barely there.

"I'm not really good at math, so I keep a pencil and paper nearby, or sometimes I do the calculation on the box or bag itself. But if you're good at math, you can just do the calculations in your head." I realize I am babbling too much, and too happily. "Um. Are you good at math?"

He shrugs.

I wish he would talk a little more. I mean, is he practicing for mime school? Still, I'm sure, despite his freaky appearance, there are lots of things we have in common. A month from now, I'll probably look back at this and laugh at myself for thinking this guy was the scariest person I'd ever met.

I hope.

All right, I give up. I have more important things to do with my life than deal with the Freaky Silent Type. Like sleep. "Yeah. Well, the price list is on the wall behind the register. If you need anything, we're upstairs. Just pick up the phone and dial one. Okay?"

I'm about to turn around when I realize that the entire lower half of his face (which is all I can see) has turned a little red. Is he blushing or choking on a piece of gum? Then his mouth opens and he says, in a tiny, fragile voice, "May I have a cupcake?"

May I have a cupcake? It's so childish, like something I'd expect a preschooler to say. Or Oliver. I can't help it: I burst out laughing.

He tilts his head to the side, obviously wondering if I'm having a convulsion.

"I'm sorry. Yeah. You can. And there's milk and juice in the fridge case. Help yourself."

He reaches into the case and pulls out a chocolate-frosted cupcake. Then he shoves the entire thing into his mouth, and in one swallow, it's gone. I can almost see the outline of it traveling down his throat, like a mouse being devoured by a snake. I gag. "Um, you can have another. Human bites, though, this time. Don't want to have to call 911 on your ass."

I laugh—it's almost a snort, but I catch myself in time—and realize that the whole "calling 911 on your ass" thing is entirely too cool for the normal Dough Reilly to say. I usually sound stiff, like a walking dictionary. I think I'm feeling emboldened by his goofy "Can I have some more, sir?" impersonation.

He takes a second one and is still chewing when he opens his mouth and says, "Thanks."

Seeing that he has kind of green teeth—and what's that? A pimple on his chin?—gives me even more courage. He's not scary at all, just a regular pussycat. I'll definitely be laughing this off by next month. "So, you're not from around here," I say, leaning over the counter.

He shakes his head and swallows, then goes over to the fridge. I expect him to expand on that, but he doesn't. He just looks out the window again, toward the Dumpster.

I figure I can have a conversation with myself, then. I'm used to being my own company. "I knew that. We don't get many new faces around here."

He wipes his mouth with the back of his hand. "I'm from out west."

Wow, first time he offered up information about himself. However, considering that we're on an island on the East Coast and just about all of the United States is out west, I can't say this is very revealing. "Cool. You mean, like, California?"

He shrugs. Scintillating conversation.

Still, he's a pussycat. A cupcake-loving little pussycat, I remind myself as I start to consolidate the donuts onto as few trays as possible, which really does not need to be done. "Anyway, you can do this, if you want," I motion to the trays. "Then put the trays in the back. The bakers wash the morning ones, but you'll have to wash all the rest after we close. It helps to keep things neat."

Suddenly, I'm aware that he's completely invaded my personal space, because I can feel his breath on my ear. I stand stick straight and swallow. "Does it matter where a person comes from," he hisses, "when they're never going back?"

Then he moves away and plucks another cupcake from the tray. I take a deep breath, and the guy goes right back to being Mr. Scary.

"**M**OM," I SAY BEFORE I've even opened the screen door to the apartment, "can you please explain to me why you thought it would be a good idea to leave your innocent daughter alone with a potential serial rapist?"

But then I realize that I'm talking to an empty room. The ledger is out on the kitchen table, and the ceiling fan has blown some of the bills onto the linoleum floor, but the plastic chair Mom usually sits in, whining and moaning, is empty.

I figure she's probably gone to the bathroom to get a tissue to blow her nose, but as I walk farther into the room, I hear it: giggling, coming from her bedroom.

If you know my mother, you know that she is the most non-giggly person on Earth. She stopped giggling, I think, a little before my dad left, and never started again. She works sixteen hours a day, so she's more of a businesslike, head-on-straight type, who only thinks of the practical. Which is why I have nothing but serviceable, lacking-any-semblance-of-style clothes to wear tomorrow. Goofing off, playing games, enjoying life—these do not exist in her world.

I stand in the doorway of her room and see her lying on her bed faceup. She's twirling the phone cord in her hand like a teenager and saying, "Oh, but you don't!" in some flirty tone I think should be reserved for paid escorts. Not moms. Ew.

Mom flirting is one of those arts that should be buried forever, like contra dancing.

But wait. Who is my mom flirting with?

She jumps up when she sees me, and her tone quickly turns businesslike. "I'll talk to you later," she says, and almost hangs up before she finishes speaking. Then she grins. "So!"

"Whatever, Mom. I'm not three. Who was that?"

"Who? Oh. The bagel deliveryman."

"You're dating the bagel delivery guy?"

She is biting her lip, kind of like a sex kitten. "What? No. I was just scheduling our deliveries for the fall season."

"And flirting."

"I was not," she says resolutely, sitting down at her ledger. "Seriously, Gwen. I am too busy to flirt. Besides, it doesn't hurt to be nice to our vendors. I don't want him blabbing all over the island that we don't bake our own bagels."

"Oo-kay," I say, even though I don't believe it. We get a

dozen bagels delivered every day and we usually end up throwing them out, because only a couple of people on the island eat them, and one of them is this senile geezer who vowed to write a letter to the governor of New Jersey decrying our establishment as anti-Semitic if we stopped supplying them. I need to let the flirting thing drop, because the fact that my mom might have a sex life is not something I want to think of right now. Actually, it's not something I want to think of ever.

Of course, not wanting to think about something is a sure way to end up thinking about it. I try to wipe the image out of my mind, but I can't remember the thing I wanted to talk to her about. Oh, right. Mr. Scary. Mr. Potential Rapist. "Um. Yeah. Why did you hire that guy? Did we officially kill off all the normal citizens of Cellar Bay? Or did he?"

She waves her hand at me. "He's fine. He's Melinda's grandson."

"He is?" I blurt out. Now that I think of it, it does totally explain why he doesn't have a decent haircut.

She nods. "I'll admit I didn't know what to expect. Melinda just told me that her grandchild, Chris, was coming to town and really needed a job to get back on his feet again. And I think I owe her a favor."

She's admiring my atrocious haircut again. I reach into the refrigerator and pull out a Vitaminwater. "Get back on his feet?"

"I don't know what she meant. It's all ancient history, anyway. And I'm not going to pry. He just came to stay with Melinda because his mother is traveling in a show."

"You mean the prostitute?"

43

"She's in show business," Mom says, correcting me, lifting her chin as if it's the noblest profession ever. Unfortunately, my mom fails to realize that most traveling show people are psychotic, restless souls, many of whom have horns growing out of their heads or other freakish characteristics that make them worthy of an audience. And any offspring of a woman who wears skintight snakeskin dresses cannot be sane. Period.

I clear my throat. "Did you get references?"

"I don't need references. Melinda is a good enough reference for me."

"But do you even know anything about him?"

"Like?"

"Like how old he is. Whether he can handle money. Whether he counts decapitating small animals as one of his hobbies."

She glares at me. "He's eighteen. And he's fine."

"But he freaks me out," I say weakly.

This comes out as a this-conversation-is-over growl: "Luckily, you will be in school and won't have to deal with him." And she turns back to her ledger.

Right. Luckily, I'll be at school. Never thought I'd be saying that.

I'M SITTING IN THE BACK of the short bus, wanting to pee my pants. Not from fear, totally. Mostly because I was late, trying to tame my triangle into a normal, human-shaped head, and trying to see if any of the outfits I owned could ever exude coolness, if accessorized correctly. Thus, before I knew it, the bus was out front, and peeing was not an option.

For the record, my hair now looks lopsided, more like a rhombus, and it's hard like a helmet, and no amount of fake jewelry can make an XXL Hanes sweatshirt look stylish.

Evie is in the front, chatting with Becca. We're the only three people on the bus. My sister is bouncing her legs up and down so that her flip-flops smack against her heels. Smack-smack-smack. She blows a noisy bubble with her gum and grins excitedly, like she's in her own musical and about to break into song.

For a second, I think maybe, maybe, maybe things won't be as bad as I've feared. Maybe when my mom and I meet Wish at the airport tonight, I can tell him about the dozens of new friends who welcomed me into their open arms and how we all sang "Kumbaya" together. Then we cross over the bridge and I see the school looming in the distance, like the house from *Psycho*. Vultures are circling over it.

Then I wake up and see the crowds of students standing outside, waiting to be let in. They're all huddled in their tight, impenetrable circles. For some reason, this reminds me of that goofy sex-ed presentation they showed in sixth grade, the one where the egg is standing firm while all these little sperm flutter about, trying to break in, constantly getting the brush-off. Yes, in this scenario, I am the sperm. Thespian egg? Denied! Chess club egg? Denied! Future Homemakers of America egg? Denied! I don't even bother to go near the really popular eggs, because that would be spermicide.

When I step from the bus, I imagine that this is how soldiers on the front lines feel when they're being shot at. I duck my head, avoid looking directly at anyone, and find a spot in a corner, near the building, where I plop down on the grass and pull out a notebook. I'll pretend to read something important in it—which is kind of difficult, since it's blank. It is the first day of school, after all. I find a pen in my purse, and the point hovers an inch over the paper for the longest time. What to write, what to write? Oh, yes. A list of things I need to bring into school with me tomorrow. Like what? I already have all the pens and notebooks I could possibly need; my ever-prepared mother had my bag packed

46

and ready to go in mid-July. I look up for a second and realize that someone—I'm not sure who—is staring at me, no
doubt thinking, "Well, well, well, what friendless loser have
we here?" and getting ready to launch an attack, so I get
nervous and write the first thing that comes to my mind.

Salami.

Where the hell did that come from? I don't even like
salami. Or anything remotely salami-like. I quickly scribble
it out, so hard that I almost rip through the page with my
pen point. Fine. I can just look through my bag for my cell
phone, like I need to make an important call. Even though
I don't actually own a cell phone.

Suddenly I hear someone yell above the noise, "Yo,
baby!"

But it isn't any ordinary "Yo, baby." It's in that horrible
nasal Rick Rothman voice. And it's really close by. I see a
pair of filthy Vans backing up toward me. Rick may be one
of the richest kids in school, but he has a way of dressing
like he's been raiding the nearest Dumpster. And he seems
always to be walking backward, tossing greetings to his
many admirers, completely oblivious to anyone who might
be in his way. I freeze.

One of his mud-crusted sneakers steps right on my new
khakis, leaving a nice footprint on my thigh. He nearly falls
back, then turns to me. His eyes trail downward. "Yo, what's
up?" he says to me, almost civilly.

How do I answer that? I could say, "Nothing," but that
makes me look like a total loser who is up to nothing, which,
even though it's true, is the last thing I want to admit. I
could tell him I'm listing lunch meats, but that's even lamer.

I could lie and say I'm writing a screenplay; that sounds cool. However, since my notebook is blank, he could easily see through that facade. A few seconds pass, and then I realize that I'm not saying anything, just staring up at him, like a deaf-mute, which is perhaps the most pathetic reaction of all. So I suddenly open my mouth and out comes this weird humming noise that sounds like a bee crash-landing on a windshield.

He doesn't notice. He's already yo-babying another bunch of girls across the green. This is probably like Christmas morning for him. I look down at the muddy footprint on my thigh as the crowd starts to funnel through the doors.

Ah, yes, school. The agony and the . . . more agony.

After making a pit stop at the girls' room, I find a seat in the back of homeroom, hoping none of the people who like to cause a scene involving me and my ass, or another of my numerous large body parts, is present. The room begins to fill up; nobody looks at me, or if they do, they quickly drop their eyes. Nobody sits by me. I'm thinking it's because I'm invisible when in walks Terra Goldbar.

Terra is a girl who thinks she's much cooler than she actually is. She has bright red hair and a horsey face, and her laugh sounds like a lawn mower starting up. She joins every club she can fit into her schedule, and so she is friends with everyone—or at least likes to think she is. Oh, except me, but I'll get to that part in a minute. It's odd to watch her change the way she acts between groups; one second she'll be discussing the works of Plato with the brains, and the next second she'll be like, "Girl! That nail polish is, like, so fabu!" to the fashion mavens. One could call her the Chameleon of Cellarton. Well, except for the stoplight hair.

Unfortunately, she's not fooling anyone. She doesn't really fit into any of the groups. For instance, her observation on Plato will be "Didn't he write that play about the guy who does it with his mother?" and the nail polish will be the most hideous fashion don't since culottes on short fat people. I think everyone keeps her around for the amusement value. Because she's so oblivious they can make fun of her and she won't get it. Because she's loyal like a puppy. Oh, and because she's freaking rich and has completely absentee parents, so she has been known to throw the most mind-blowing parties Cellarton High has ever seen.

She tosses her Gucci bag down on the floor beside the farthest possible empty desk from mine. Since the room is pretty full, it's a desk kitty-corner to mine, so close she can reach out and touch me. Still, she pretends not to notice me, turns to Erica Dunleavy in the next row, and says, way too bubbly for this early in the morning, "Hey, girl! You got a new tat! Fabuloso!"

So here's why, out of all the students at Cellarton High, Terra picked me as the object of her wrath. She and Wish are cousins. More than just cousins. She writes comments on his Facebook wall at least once a day, usually starting with "Hey, favorite cousin!" And no "favorite cousin" of hers should associate with the likes of me. I think she's disgusted with me because in all my years, I've never had a birthday with a petting zoo, or a bat mitzvah with a robot fortune-teller. Even though his Facebook page says "In a Relationship

49

with Gwendolyn Reilly," she doesn't get it. Maybe she thinks Gwendolyn Reilly is a figment of his imagination. If I ever went up to her and told her that Wish was my boyfriend, she'd probably have one of those brain meltdowns and start sputtering, "Does not compute! Does not compute!" So she has done well all these years just pretending I don't exist.

I look over to see them both admiring a purple blotch on the top of Erica's foot, right under the strap of her white flip-flops. Erica has this rough-voiced, mysterious, Harley-riding sex-kitten thing going for her, which means she is my polar opposite. And she's had a reputation since before I stopped playing with Barbies. There was a rumor going around sixth grade that her father had come home one afternoon and found Erica making out with her new boyfriend, topless. I can almost believe it, because even though we were only twelve then, Erica already had the kind of rack one wouldn't mind showing off.

She says, "Yeah, I got it from a local when we went to Fiji. It means 'peaceful journey.' "

Is it wrong that I hope the local gave her a symbol that means "I have to pee" instead? Or "spoiled rich American teen hoochie"? I start to giggle to myself; then I have to stifle a snort. I guess I don't suppress it well enough, because Terra turns to glare at me. Well, at least she acknowledged that I exist.

"Oh, hey," she says to Erica, talking a mile a minute. "Did you hear about Wish?"

Obviously, seeing me has sparked the mysterious Dough-Wish connection in Terra's brain. Erica nods, and for a second my heart does a free fall. I knew it was a lost cause hoping that when he came to school, nobody would remember him, that he would be just another faceless nobody like me. After all, though he hasn't been around in four years, he still knows the people of Cellarton High better than I do, judging by all the messages they leave on his Facebook wall. But Erica? She can barely remember her own name. This is not a good sign. "Yeah, where is he? I thought he'd be here."

"His plane got delayed or something," Terra says. "He's coming in tonight."

Erica gives one of her famous sly grins. "I can't wait to see him. He looks so hot in his pictures."

I slide down in my seat. Well, yeah, four years ago, Wish was awkward and gangly, and the pictures of him now are a definite improvement. There was no question in my mind that Wish would be higher-shelf than me. But he's not supposed to be right there on the top! If Erica, gorgeous Erica, thinks he's hot, what does that mean for me? My best hope now is that he got glamour shots taken of him out in L.A. that make him look extremely hot, but in reality he is a puny little booger with acne and bad breath. How pathetic am I that I want a boyfriend with bad breath?

Terra flips her red hair. "I wanted to see if anyone would come with me to meet him at the airport tonight. As a welcome-back surprise. So far I have like twenty people. You coming?"

Erica nods. "Why not?"

Wait, wait. No. My mom and I were going to meet Wish at the airport. That was the plan. I'd imagined the whole thing: Wish hurrying up the ramp with a bag slung over his shoulder, then dropping it and running for me. He would take me in his arms and twirl me around. Okay, maybe not twirl me, but just pick me up. Okay, maybe not pick me up, but give me one momentary heave-ho so that my sandals fell off and my cute little pedicure, the only thing cute about me, showed. Airport lighting makes people look like the dead, yes, but there was a chance he'd be so jet-lagged he'd think Mrs. Potato Head was hot. And maybe if I shoved my feet in his face, first thing, he would be so mesmerized that everything north of them wouldn't matter.

Terra goes right on ignoring me, making plans to pick Erica up at whatever time tonight, and meanwhile, my first twinge of disappointment fades and I'm left feeling . . . relieved. Because if they're going to be his welcome committee, I don't need to be. And if I don't go, then I won't see Wish tonight. And if I don't see Wish, I don't have to worry about my biggest fear: his face distorting in anguish as he screams, "No, *no!* You ate my Gwen!"

Which is actually more believable than his being able to pick me up and twirl me through the airport like I'm Julie Andrews.

My breath catches when I hear Erica say, "He's not going with anyone, is he?"

And here's the best part: Terra shrugs and says, "No, not that I know of."

I didn't expect her to say, "Why, yes, I hear he's with her," and point me out. I mean, maybe she really doesn't know who I am.

But then she says, "He never talks about anyone, anyway."

Hello? What part of "In a Relationship with Gwendolyn Reilly" is in any way unclear?

Maybe Terra is just saying that he never talks about me to rip my little heart to pieces, but part of me also thinks it could be true. Maybe Wish never does talk about me. But why would he, to someone who hardly knows I exist? Seriously, Dough, in his past few emails he's been so excited to see you, I tell myself. He even had a little countdown of the hours and minutes and seconds in there, like a total nerd. He's not ashamed of you. Not yet, anyway.

The imprint of Rick's sneaker on my thigh looks even darker now. I rub at it, but it doesn't help. Not that it matters. I'm probably going to get stepped on a lot more today, so I might as well get used to it.

9

ON THE WAY HOME, I have the bus to myself. Well, I do have a companion; I'm sitting with my stack of books, which seems to have a life all its own. It's a good thing I'm not going to the airport tonight, because I have so much home-work that I couldn't fit everything in my backpack and had to carry some books in my arms, which nearly killed me. I made it to the bus, huffing and puffing, but the bus driver didn't see me. She closed the doors on me, and now I have two black marks on my shoulders from the rubber. Evie and Becca are nowhere to be found, meaning two things: 1) they found some seniors to give them a ride home, and 2) I am officially the only living dork on the island of Cellar Bay.

Other than that, my first day of school was everything I'd expected. In class, nobody talked to me, and everyone attempted to sit as far away from me as possible. During lunch, one lost freshman tried to sit at my table, but three other freshmen pulled her from the brink before it was too late. "Don't do it!" they cried. "You still have worth! People still love you! We have a seat over here!" She heaved an enormous sigh of relief and scurried off to join them. Things could have been worse, though, I tell myself.

I'm trying to think of how when the bus pulls up outside the bakery, and I can already tell that we have no customers. Through the glass, I can see the outline of someone— probably that dude Christian, leaning against the counter, looking bored. I'm thinking I should have shown him a couple of things he can do—folding boxes, refilling the cookie trays, sweeping the floor—when he doesn't have anything else to do. As I'm climbing off the bus, a little fearful that the doors are going to close on me again, which kind of hurt, I drop my brand-new trig book. It falls into the gutter, open, where there's a small river of sandy water from last night's rain. As I rush to pick it up and minimize the damage, I see behind me a small flash of fire-engine red from someone's car. Someone's really nice car. I turn, because it's impossible to avoid looking at a car that's that tiny and sporty and sleek, if only to see what idiot would buy a mode of transportation that has absolutely no storage, no passenger room, and no traction in bad weather. Oh my God, I fully realize I am turning into my mother.

Beyond the glistening BMW hood ornament, I see a waterfall of equally shiny blond hair. Evie's. She's sitting in the passenger seat, giggling spinelessly at the driver.

I drop my books again.

I knew it.

I knew it.

I knew it.

I stand there for a moment, holding my breath. Then I pick up my books and run into the bakery, only to throw them down again on the linoleum. Then I scream. Scream like there's no tomorrow. Scream every curse word, in every odd combination I can think of, until I'm red in the face and want to puke. Christian just watches me, squinting.

Finally, I calm down. I'm still breathing hard, but my voice lowers a few octaves. "Sorry," I say. "You see, that guy out there . . . I sort of . . . 'Hate' is too nice a word."

I don't know, was I expecting a reaction from a guy who has yet to utter more than three syllables to me? Because he just stares at me, looking confused.

"That girl out there. She's my sister. And she's only fourteen. And obviously stupid." I clench my fists and let out a growl. "Is English your second language? 'Cause you're really starting to get on my nerves."

It kind of just slipped out. I guess that fear I harbored, the one of his maybe stabbing my heart with the butter knife, has been trumped by the fear of having to sing "Itsy Bitsy Spider" to a little Rothman niece or nephew.

He clears his throat. I wait eagerly for his words, though I'm not sure why. Was I expecting this stoner dude to hold the key to the universe? "She's your sister?" he finally asks, clearly shocked.

I sigh. "I know. It goes against the laws of nature that two completely opposite-looking creatures can be related by blood. I get that."

He shakes his head. "What the hell is a scumbling screwfinger?"

I stare at him, dumbfounded. I vaguely recall those words escaping my lips during my vent. My inventory of expletives could probably use some work.

He's still looking out the window. "Are you jealous?"

"Of course not. That guy's a jerk. And I have a boyfriend." At least, for the time being. "He's been in California for a few years, but he's . . ." My voice trails off when I realize I'm explaining something to someone who should not matter. Why is it that suddenly all the things that never seemed to matter in my life do?

He nods, looking unconvinced.

"What?" I demand. I mean, what did he mean by that? It's her right to spend time with jerks if she so chooses. Okay, yeah, maybe I was a little bit sore about having to take the bus home while my younger sister got a ride, but I was not jealous of who she had to spend that entire ride home with. It would be like riding home with nails screeching across a chalkboard. "Why would I be jealous?"

He shrugs. "Because I am. That's a sweet ride."

I think I liked him better when he didn't talk.

I growl again, then gather my mountain of books and run upstairs. My mom is nowhere to be found. I'm so eager to get my sister in trouble that I call, "Ma?" over and over through the apartment. I hear a faint "Hi, hon" echoing, but can't tell where it's coming from. Sounds like she's stuffed in a closet, under a pile of clothes. I throw everything in my arms onto my bed and turn on my computer.

There's an email from Wish that must have come last night, after I'd gone to sleep. More of his goofy countdown: *00:20:04:36! CAN'T WAIT!!!*

Then I find my mother lying on the floor of the living room. At first I think she's trying to do push-ups, which is something my mother never, ever does, since she runs around like crazy all day baking and has the physique of a matchstick. Then I realize she's Swiffering under the couch. She cleans like a madwoman.

"Ma, did you see what Evie is doing—"

She picks her head up. "Hi, hon. How was school?"

I hold up my hand and beckon her to the front window. "Glorious. Mom. Look. Look what Evie is doing."

She pulls the cloth off the Swiffer and smiles at all the dust she's collected, then dips one of the slats of our metal blinds and peers outside. "Wow. Nice car."

"Ma, that's Rick. He's way older than her. And a jerk to the highest power."

She nods, very seriously. "Wow. In what way?"

"You know, full of himself. Player."

I think she's going to whip down the stairs and drag Evie from the car by her hair. Instead, she starts to chew on her pinky fingernail. "Nice car."

Frustrated, I look out the window myself. They've some-how moved closer together. I can hear Evie's girly "a-hee-a-hee-a-hee" from here. She sounds like an asthmatic donkey. "He's two secs away from swallowing her head."

"You think?" She doesn't sound very concerned.

"Aren't you going to do anything?"

"Like drag her from the car by her hair?"

I shrug. Well, why not? "She's only fourteen."

She smiles at me. "Thank you, Love Police." Then she turns back toward her Swiffer. "They're only talking. You'll probably be doing a lot worse tonight."

I realize, at that moment, how completely out of it she is. No, I won't. I have morals. I have dignity. I have a body that, when unclothed, scares even my shower curtain. My mouth hangs open. My own mother is encouraging me to get nasty with my boyfriend. Aren't there laws against that?

She runs a dust cloth over the TV, then inspects the tiny room. "What do you think? Good enough for the honorable Mr. Wishman?"

It takes me a moment to realize that this was a special psychotic cleaning binge. She did it for my boyfriend. "Um."

"We'd better leave for the airport soon, hmm?" she asks, checking the clock.

"Change in plans. He's coming in late," I fib. "After midnight. So I'll just see him at school tomorrow, I guess."

She closes her lips. "Oh. Bummer."

I take one last look out the window. Rick now has his arm around Evie and is playing with her hair.

So today is a red-letter day. The day my sister gets involved with her first scum-sucking pig. The day my boyfriend, who I haven't seen in years, comes back to town. And the day I'll be doing trigonometry until my head falls off. Perfection.

10

I'M SITTING AT THE LIVING ROOM coffee table, drinking Diet Coke, half watching *Oprah* and half trying to determine what sine is and what relevance it has in my life. I hate math; Wish is a math geek. If he were here, he'd laugh at me and say, in a very Buddha-like way, "Duh, Gwen. The answer is twelve," without even having to think.

As I'm about to burst into tears, Evie saunters in. Again she looks like she's going to break into song.

I push my pencil against my notebook so hard that the tip almost breaks. "Your ever-so-dreamy new boyfriend is a turd," I say, not looking up.

She practically floats into the overstuffed chair across from me. "He is not my boyfriend," she says, not very convincingly at all.

"I'll give it a week before he is."

She clicks her tongue. "Dough, I'm not an idiot. I remember what happened last week. I know what he's like."

"Then why were you . . ."

"I've always wanted a ride in a BMW. But that's all he's good for. Seriously." And she gives me this wholesome grin, the heart-melting kind. "I've got your back, girl."

Since Evie has never done anything really trashy to me before, I guess I have to believe her. However, she's new to guys, and as I've learned, girls can do some pretty warped things for guys. I've known normal, sweet girls who've fought like mad lions over men. Stranger things have happened. "So you're seriously telling me you're never ever going to see him again?"

She raises her eyebrows. "Well, that's impossible. He's in study hall with me, and—"

"He's driving you to school tomorrow, isn't he?"

"Well, yeah," she says, biting her lower lip. "I'd rather be caught dead than in that little bus." She thinks for a moment and then says, "Oh. No offense."

I roll my eyes. "Well, just take it from someone who's older. Don't get too close. Guys can bite. And by the time they do, you're the one wearing the dog collar."

She wrinkles her pert nose. "What does that mean? It's pretty nice of him to agree to come all the way over from his winter home on the mainland to pick me and Becca up."

"He should apply for sainthood," I agree.

She cranes her neck to look at the clock, then sits up straight. "Well, I've got to jet. I need to get a shower in."

I scowl at her. "Are you going out with him tonight?"

"Arf, arf," she says, pretending to beg like a puppy. "No dog collars here. It isn't just with him. It's a group thing."

"You're going to a party on the first night of school?"

"It's not a party," she says. "At least, I don't think it is. He said something about going to the Airport. Like, a bunch of people are going to hang out there. I think it's the name of a new restaurant or something. It can't be the real airport, like where planes and stuff come in, right?"

I shrug and suddenly want to stab myself in the eye with my pencil. My own sister is going to be welcoming Wish back to Jersey tonight, and I won't be there. Who knows, maybe they'll have a parade and strippers and fireworks, too. I wonder if, with all the fanfare, he'll even care that I'm not there.

11

THAT NIGHT, I can't sleep. I have these two competing visions in my mind: one of Wish trying to find me among his horde of admirers, then bursting into tears when he realizes I'm not there, and shouting to the heavens, "Why, God, why?" And the other of him being tackled by a crowd of hot, naked cheerleaders as soon as he comes up the ramp.

A little after eleven, I hear voices on the street below, and then a car door slams and footsteps quickly but lightly ascend the rickety staircase outside. Evie. When the door swings open, I almost tackle her in the kitchen, in the dark. She lets out a little scream and then I realize I must look like a complete psychopath, jumping on my sister like that. So I cover up by whispering, "Oh, sorry. I forgot you were out. I thought you were a burglar."

She takes a deep breath, recovering. "Who the hell would want to steal from this place?"

"Sorry," I say. "So, how were things?"

"Fine." She yawns and makes a move like she's going to head to her bedroom, and I jump in front of her, nearly tripping over our kitchen table.

"Where are you going?"

"To pee, and then bed," she says.

It's late, and I'm tired, too, but the only thing I'm fully aware of is that if I have to go to bed without getting the lowdown on what happened tonight from her, I will not live through the night. I grab her by the wrist, open the fridge, and say, "You want something to eat?"

She yawns again. "God, no."

I slam the refrigerator door and stand there, blocking her from the bathroom. "Um, so, really, did you have a good time?"

She shrugs. "Look, you have nothing to worry about with Rick. I don't even think he's my type."

"I don't care about that," I say, which is true, for the moment. Right now, all I want to know is whether Wish got naked with some pom-pom-wielding harlots. "Like, so did that new restaurant have good food?"

She laughs. "Oh, get this! It wasn't a restaurant. We actually went to the Philly airport. To see Wish. So why weren't you there?"

At least it occurred to her that I should have been part of the welcoming party for my boyfriend. "Well," I say, "I thought it would be overwhelming, so many people there . . ."

"You got that right. It was a madhouse. I think the whole school was there."

Except me. Great; my boyfriend, the celebrity.

"Oh. How does he look?"

She nods. "Good. Really good."

I'm not sure why I asked that. Evie isn't the best at description. Everything looks good or fine or okay to her. Fishing for information with her is about as fun and easy as clothes shopping for me. "Did he . . . say anything to you?"

"I didn't really talk to him. He was kind of busy."

Busy. Since getting Evie to elaborate is impossible, all kinds of meanings for "busy" fill my mind. Busy trying to find his luggage at baggage claim. Busy signing autographs. Busy having sex with a cheerleader behind the Auntie Anne's pretzel stand. I realize I've gnawed the inside of my lower lip to a bloody pulp, so I start working on the upper.

"He had to get home early, too," she continues. "He was kind of in a rush. Only stayed a few minutes."

"Oh?" I ask, my mood brightening.

"Can I pee now?" she asks, waving me aside.

"Freely," I sigh.

I walk to the living room and peer out the blinds. I don't know what I'm looking for. Maybe I'm hoping he'll pull a Romeo and appear beneath me. He used to do that before, when we were kids, just show up and throw pebbles at my window, at all hours of the day, because the rickety staircase to our door sways pretty badly and always freaked him out. When all I see is a circle of the empty sidewalk below, illuminated by one buzzing streetlamp, and my queer, confused expression reflected in the glass, I finally trudge off to bed.

12

THE NEXT DAY, when the alarm goes off, I feel like there's a fifty-pound weight on my chest. It's not easy to pull myself up. Finally, I do, then turn on the light and rifle through my drawers until I find my only pair of semi-cool jeans and a frilly white blouse my mother bought me to wear "only for special occasions." I figure meeting my boyfriend for the first time counts as a special occasion. I spent all night mentally going through my closet and drawers, and this is what I decided on. I'm hoping against hope that if I wear it unbuttoned at the neck, with jeans and flip-flops, it will look very peasanty and flattering. Either that or I will look like a tool in a frilly church-lady blouse.

When I've dressed and sufficiently tamed my hair (this time it's more of a trapezoid), I stuff an Eggo into my mouth and find Evie peering out the living room blinds. "Hey," she says. "I forgot to tell you. I asked Rick, and he said it would be cool if you came with us."

Just what I needed. Charity from my little sister. I give her a small snarl. "I'd rather walk."

She gives me a "suit yourself" shrug. "He's trying to be nice."

"Ev, I think the terminology he used was 'lard.' You were there."

"He didn't mean to," she says.

"I'm sure it was just a slip of the tongue. He probably meant to say 'sex goddess' instead."

She exhales. "I think he's trying to change. He's being nice."

"Because he wants to get into my sister's pants."

She gives me a confused look and begins to launch into a protest but then turns to the window. "Your ride is here."

Holding my chin up as high as I can, I grab my bag and walk out the door. I might as well be riding to school in a giant inflatable hot dog. Still, as I climb aboard, I'm just happy the bus driver doesn't close the doors on me. Though I'm the only passenger on the bus, I'm glad. Nobody can see my nervous breakdown. Except, of course, the bus driver. She keeps staring over the gold rims of her *Top Gun* sunglasses, into the rearview mirror, at me. Probably thinking, Is it any wonder she's the only person on the island who doesn't have an alternative method of transportation? She can barely breathe, much less carry on a social life.

The end of the trip comes too quickly for my liking. Out the grimy window, I see the normal tight circles of students everywhere on the green, waiting to be let in. I scan the crowd quickly, hoping to find Wish's head, to see him before he sees me. I don't. I see Terra there, talking to a bunch of jocks, and throngs of other people I'm not friends with. But no Wish.

Maybe he isn't here. Maybe he decided to take the day off, to recover from the jet lag. That's possible, right?

Then I realize I'm hyperventilating. The obnoxious bus driver clears her throat loudly, as if to say, "Get off now." For a second I want to command her to close the doors and drive, drive anywhere, but she's not my limo service. Shark pit, here I come.

I step down the stairwell, but suddenly the doors almost fly closed, right on my face. The bus driver laughs sadistically. "Just kidding, hon!" she cries as I turn and glare at her. I wish she would save her warped sense of humor for a day when I'm not about to vomit all over myself.

My flip-flops touch down on the sidewalk and I look at them like they're alien feet. They're ever so cute, but they can't belong to my body. My body would have had the sense to stay home today. To stay home forever.

My heart is drumming out a Sousa march. I plaster a fake-confident smile on my face and carefully navigate around a few people, whose backs are to me. A girl in one tight circle runs her fingers through her long hair, and they catch on a knot at the very end so that when she pulls her hand loose, she does it with such force that she accidentally scrapes my cheek with her vulture claws. Ouch, ouch, ouch! It's like someone sliced my cheek with a razor blade. She turns, smiling, as if to say, "Sorry," but then decides not to when she realizes it's just me. I rub the skin over my mouth, then inspect my fingers. Blood. The hoochie with the fingernails of death has drawn blood. Drawn blood and not even apologized.

And it isn't just a little scratch. I feel something wet sliding down my chin, a few drops collecting there before diving off onto the concrete. As I'm searching through my bag for a tissue, I tilt my head, so the blood starts to slide down my neck, onto my frilly white blouse. Were those fingernails or miniature chain saws?

I clamp the tissue over my cheek, but not soon enough. A few people notice. They break out of the circles, not to offer me a Band-Aid, but to gawk. Even the girl with the mongo fingernails turns to look, batting her eyelashes innocently, as if she has no idea what happened. "Um," someone says, tugging on my sleeve. I turn to see a cute freshman, wide-eyed, innocent, giving me a wholesome, friendly Noxzema-faced grin.

Finally, someone to offer a nice word. "Yes?"

She points to my middle. "Your fly is open."

I look down. It isn't just my fly that's open. That would be an easy fix. Below my frilly blouse, my jeans are sitting there, wide open, on my hips. You can see my orange underwear. A flashback of Wish seeing my peace undies in the restroom of the Cellarton Country Club floods my mind. The tissue in my hand flutters to the floor and I hoist the jeans up toward my waist, then try to button them. But I can't. The button must have popped off somewhere. And without that button, the zipper can't hold the fort. Without that button, the pants are doomed to go the way of the Alamo.

Little freshman goes back to her group, but they're still all laughing and whispering. By then, I have a bit of an audience. A few more drops of blood hit the pavement. I clasp together my pants with one hand, then lean over to grab the tissue I dropped. Because my books are so heavy, I nearly topple forward as I do, and force myself right into the middle of one of the closed circles, one of the only closed circles that heretofore had been unaware of my existence.

"Gwen?"

It's almost like a beam of sunlight falls upon me before I even raise my head, because I begin to feel warm and feverish at once. I close my eyes. Oh, no. No. No. No.

I take a breath. Another. And straighten. And turn toward him.

"Um. Hi."

13

THE MORNING AIR of early September is cool, but my face is all asizzle. My body starts to ache, starting with a pounding in my head. I hear some voices, a little laughter in my ears, but I can't tell if the titters are directed at me. My vision is blurred, and I can't lift my eyes from a lopsided smiley face that my blood has made on the cement between my feet. Even my own bodily fluids seem to find the humor in this situation.

"Damn, Gwen, are you okay?" His voice is a lot smoother in person, when it's not distorted by the crackle of the phone. I still can't bring myself to look at him, but I feel his hand on the sleeve of my blouse. He gently tugs me toward an empty bench and sits me down. "What happened?"

I'm still holding on to my pants for dear life. When I sit,

I let them go and, saying a prayer of thanks for my having worn a loose, flowy shirt with lots of extra material, billow my blouse out in front of me so that my undies don't show. Then I stare at my lap, trying to muster up the courage to peek at him. Meanwhile, I feel my temperature rising, the back of my neck burning as if it's against an open flame. I don't think I can live if I see disappointment in his face. Finally, I do it. I look up.

Just for a second.

And it's him, but not him. Not the Wish I knew way back when. The eyes are the same shape, the nose, too, but everything else is foreign. I've seen this Wish in pictures, but pictures never convey a whole person. He has more definition to his jawline, light stubble on his chin, and a perfectly even California tan. His skin is exquisite—it almost looks airbrushed—which is weird considering that when he left four years ago, he was already starting to get acne. Now he looks like he doesn't even have pores. Maybe if I squint just right, I can see past the golden aura surrounding him. Maybe, somewhere, I can find the geeky boy from elementary school. Please?

"I got . . . mauled," I say, pointing to my face. I'm about to point to my stomach and my problem there, but I stop myself. Do I really want him looking at my stomach? "And, um, having a wardrobe malfunction."

"Do you need stitches?" he asks. "Here. Let me see."

A couple of guys from his group, who were gawking at the whole sordid incident, turn away. One slaps him on the back and says, "See you, man." Wish gives a nod, gently places his hand on the bloody tissue clamped onto my face, then puts a finger on my chin. I flinch; his touch feels like a red-hot poker. "Ouch."

He quickly removes his hand and gives me a sheepish look. "Oh. Sorry."

People begin to filter through the doors, and I still can't look at him. I look up, at one of the downspouts coming off the roof of the school. It is badly in need of repair and obviously very exciting. Then I look at his shirt. It's a long-sleeved black oxford, buttoned all the way up to the neck. Since it's still eighty degrees out, that's kind of weird, but who am I to talk about weirdness? He's sitting beside me, so close, looking at the scratch on my face, but I can't look any higher than the collar of his shirt. Why can't I look at him?

"It's stopped bleeding," he says, crumpling the tissue in his hand. "As for the wardrobe malfunction . . ."

"I have shorts in my gym locker," I say, eyes fastened on the dingy gray brickwork outside the building. "I can get them after homeroom."

"You have a shirt, too?" he asks, his finger moving toward me. At first I think he's going to touch me with his red-hot-poker fingers, which will likely make me pee my pants, but instead he just points at my arm, where a couple of quarter-sized bloodstains are already starting to turn brown on my white blouse.

"Oh. Yeah."

"Okay, then. Cool. Everything else okay? What's up with your eye?"

I think one of them might be twitching from the stress.

Great, I look totally insane; I might as well wear my back-pack on my head and start bock-bock-bocking like a chicken and complete the picture. I blink. "Nothing."

"It's good to see you," he says brightly. "Finally."

"Oh, I know," I say, even though I'm really not doing much "seeing" of him. "I . . ."

He moves closer to me, maybe coming in for a hug. It nearly makes me jump off the bench. This is all incredibly weird. I slide off the seat, clutching my hands over my mid-section to keep my pants up. "I'd better get to homeroom," I say, but my mouth feels thick and numb, so it comes out like "hummer rum." Kill me now.

"Wait, when can we compare schedules? Do we have any classes together?" He springs up next to me, and I realize how tall he's gotten. He could probably rest his chin on the top of my head. This is a good thing; I can look at his chest instead of into his face, since that's what's at eye level. But how did his chest get to be so big? Beyond the shirt that used to hang lifelessly over his bony limbs are . . . muscles?

Okay, yeah. I was expecting him to be hot. I knew he'd be out of my league. But I don't think anything could have prepared me for this. Even if I were still my skinny old self, I'd be self-conscious. Wish isn't just hot. He's beautiful.

And even stranger, he hasn't yet run away screaming from me. He wants to compare schedules with me. As in see me again.

Which, for some reason, makes me want to run away screaming from him.

"Um. After homeroom?" I enunciate the word slowly, like I'm learning to pronounce it for the first time.

He nods. "Yeah. I'll meet you outside the girls' locker room."

I expect him to finish that off with a "Not!" but he doesn't. He just stands there, and as I'm beginning to believe that this is an imposter, not my best friend, he begins to fidget. I'd know the Wish Fidget anywhere; it's goofy and awkward and always used to make me laugh, but somehow, on this version of Wish, it's ultra-adorable. I try to look up to his eyes, but only make it as far as the brown sugar stubble on his chin before I chicken out. Wish has stubble. Wish has become a full-grown god, while I've become a logo for snack cakes.

We stand there for a moment longer, both kind of fidgeting now, and then I realize something. What was the first thing he wanted to do when he saw me? The thing he's been waiting for all these years?

Oh, hell.

I start to hyperventilate. My breath is sweet with maple syrup, from the Eggo I had earlier today. Guess it could be worse. But since yesterday, I've gnawed my lips to sandpaper.

"Um, yeah," I mutter. It must be the most awkward parting line in history. Then I just turn and waddle away, dragging my pants and packed bag of books with me.

14

MY PINK SWEAT SHORTS are only slightly better than my popped-open jeans with a window to my undies. They're hopelessly tight, clinging to the folds around my hips like plastic wrap over Silly Putty. My legs poke out of them like two buffet lines filled with nothing but cottage cheese. I'm not sure what Wish was thinking earlier when he met me outside, but maybe there was sun glare or his sense of reason was thrown off by the six-hour plane ride. Of course, when he sees me looking like an aerobics instructor who accidentally Botoxed her butt, he will probably come to his senses.

I step outside, yanking the shorts down as far as I possibly can manage without allowing my stomach to spring free of the waistband. These shorts give me a major crotch wedgie. Yes, this will make Wish wake up. There is no man alive who can be turned on by a crotch wedgie.

I see him down the hallway. Actually, I don't see him; I just see the burnt orange shock of hair that belongs to him peeking out from the middle of a crowd of girls. Well, not exactly a crowd, but three. As I get closer, I realize that two of them are Erica and Terra. There's also a girl named Destiny, who bears an uncanny resemblance to Barbie, right down to the skinny waist that cannot possibly hold all the required internal organs. Terra whinnies loudly, her horse nostrils flaring. Erica stares up at Wish with sultry, "take me now" eyes. Wish isn't really looking at them; he's telling them about his eventful plane ride and is completely into his story, gesturing with both hands in classic Wish fashion. He could always spin a great yarn. But he'd always been the funny Mr. Personality, not Mr. GQ. Still, as I get closer, I can almost make out a little glistening something in the corner of Erica's mouth.

I stand outside the circle, ready to bolt down the hall, when Wish notices me. There's no sun glare or bad lighting or large objects in the way or anything whatsoever that would stop him from seeing me in all my chunky glory, but contrary to what I was expecting, no disgust registers on his face. "Oh, hey, Gwen, what's the name of that place in Princeton? Where we used to get the ice cream?"

Three sets of eyes turn in unison to glare at me. And is it me, or do they all narrow to evil slits?

"Um. Thomas Sweet," I squeak, remembering when his mother, who was working on her thesis, would take us up there on Saturdays. We would walk around the campus, eating giant vanilla Blend-Ins with M&M's and Butterfinger and Oreo pieces until we nearly puked. I'm kind of flattered that he can remember it, that he can think of anything at all with Erica's sex eyes focused on him.

"Right. So yeah, they make the best ice cream. Like, sell-your-mother-for-it good. And then this guy in the seat next to me says . . ."

Wish yanks me into the circle, where I stand like an uneven table. At that point I lose track of the story. I lose track of pretty much everything, including how to breathe, because I begin to hyperventilate again. I have no idea what the bridge was between his plane ride here and Thomas Sweet, but I don't care. Those three sets of eyes keep trailing toward me, running over the length of my body, narrowing and widening whenever they stop on my goose-pimply white legs. Clearly, I have invaded their circle. The story seems to go on forever; then finally he gets to the punch line and the girls laugh at him like they're on speed. I muster a few polite "heh's."

Then, suddenly, all four sets of eyes trail back to me. Uncomfortable silence sets in.

"Hey!" Wish says, pulling me to his side like I'm his bookend. "You guys know Gwen, don't you?"

Erica and Destiny mumble yeses, and Terra blurts out the sunniest, fakest "Oh, yeah, hey!" She reaches over and swipes her ice-cold hand over my arm as if she's flicking dust from it. "What's up?"

Nobody seems to notice the irony. Wish, who has been

away for years, introducing me. Me. As if he's been here all along and I just arrived from Planet Fat.

More uncomfortable silence. Finally, Wish says something like "I'll catch you later," and the girls head down the hallway, whispering, shoulders touching. I am sure words like "hottie" and "gorgeous" are being freely batted about.

I turn toward Wish and he's looking at me. Again, I dart my eyes away. "You okay?" he asks.

He probably keeps asking that because I look anything but. "Great," I mutter.

He reaches into the pocket of his baggy pants and pulls out a folded sheet of paper. "Your schedule?"

"Oh." I search clumsily through my bag and pull it out. There are a crushed Skittle and one of my mousy brown hairs attached to it, but I pick them off and hand it over.

He studies the papers. For a minute I think he must be carefully deciding how to diplomatically tell his hippo girlfriend to buzz off, but then he says, "Cool! We have lunch together." Then he shrugs. "Nothing else, though. Why do you have to be so smart?"

"Er . . ." I'm so smart that speech escapes me. "You're in honors precalc; I'm in honors English."

See? I'm not smarter, just different.

"Still, lunch is good."

Oh, sure, lunch is just great. After sitting alone for the entire period yesterday, I planned to eat the rest of my lunches in the music wing bathroom. Now Wish will probably encourage me to sit with Terra and Erica and other people I clearly don't fit in with, and they'll likely spend the entire time watching me and my cheese sandwich and wondering why we infiltrated their lofty domain. My sandwich and I would much prefer the company of a toilet.

"Well, I'd better get going to English for Dummies. You'd better get going to . . ." He checks my schedule. "Ooh. Creative writing. Write a poem about me, okay?"

I stand there in my little shorts, dumbfounded. Why is he acting like there's nothing wrong with this picture? Like everything's exactly as we left it?

He clears his throat, then looks down at his shirt and adjusts his cuffs as if he's self-conscious. Then he grins at me, and for the second time today, my eyes briefly meet his. Gorgeous as they are, there's something not right about them. Somehow it seems like he's not all there. Like he's looking through me.

But he has to see it. Has to. Right?

15

AT LUNCH, I skulk through the cafeteria doors late. I purposely spent a few extra minutes at my locker, because I didn't want to get there first and have Wish see everyone whizzing around to avoid me like I'm a smoking car in the breakdown lane. The moment I walk in, Wish waves to me with both arms. He's excited to see me. How can that be? Do I have season passes to the Flyers stapled to my forehead or something?

I am acutely aware that the farther away I am from him, the more obvious my cottage-cheese legs are in this horrid fluorescent light. They're like a beacon in the night. If he's standing right next to me, it's harder for him to see them. So that's why I sprint over to him, like Jesse Owens. It's only a short trip, but I'm still out of breath by the time I get there.

"There" is a table right in the center of the commotion, where people who don't mind being seen like to sit. I never venture there. Yet here I am, in all my goose-pimply glory, being given the once-over by two long rows of popular kids. Erica is there, and a bunch of hot guys who don't know I exist. And—oh, great. Perfect. Rick. He's farther down the row, surrounded by girls, and he's the only one besides Wish who doesn't seem ready to puke because of my presence. Probably because he's too busy telling a story to his entourage, likely involving himself and his awesomeness.

"Hey, what's up?" Wish asks casually.

"Um, nothing." I'm clutching my books so close to my chest that I think my skin might absorb them and they'll get stuck in my intestines.

He looks around, and I can tell he's trying to find a seat for me. Nope, no seat. No dice. Guess I'll just keep my date with the toilet. No biggie.

Then, before I know it, he grabs my sleeve and I lose my balance for a second but end up awkwardly plopping into his lap. But not really into it. I don't fit neatly into anything. I kind of sit there on one of his knees, balancing precariously. I can't believe it. I am going to cripple my boyfriend on his very first full day back east.

I can tell that people around the table are just as flabbergasted as I am. Their eyes widen even farther than when the goose-pimply fatty showed up at their table. Erica turns toward the windows, like she's watching her sterling, geek-free reputation fluttering out of them.

Wish wraps his arms around my fat and pulls me closer,

as if he isn't in the worst pain of his life. He laughs, and his voice is completely unstrained when he says, "There. Problem solved."

I shyly inspect the people at the table. One of the hot guys who usually ignore me—named Fudge, shortened from DeFuca a while back—half grins. At me. Meaning he sees me. "Zup?" he asks coolly.

There is no way, ever, ever, ever, that my cheese sandwich is going to see the outside of my bag. Not in this company. I feel hot again, faint. Like if I never eat again, it will be too soon.

Another one of the hottest guys on the planet—somehow sexy besides his being completely bald except for one long braid sprouting from the side of his head, and having the nickname Skull—leans toward me. He gives me an intense look, and for a moment I think he might lunge across the table and kill me. Instead, he just nods and says, "Word."

"So, yeah. You in on Friday?" Fudge asks. He's looking at me. He can't be talking to me, though, right? Up until now, I was pretty sure he couldn't see me. And who wouldn't be in on Friday? It's a school day, isn't it? It's not a school-optional day. Or maybe it is, but just for the cool people.

Wish leans over. "Party at Terra's. Friday night. Want to go?"

I feel his breath on my cheek. So he's talking either to me or to some invisible thing on my shoulder. I've never been part of the social scene at Cellarton, not even the lame poker parties the math club has on Fridays. But these guys are all looking at me as if I belong there. So I smile and nod and try to play it cool. My bare knees are knocking together, so I thrust my hand between them to steady them.

At that moment, it comes to my attention that I haven't breathed in a very long time. I exhale as the guys resume their normal conversation, about the Eagles and how they need to step it up this year if they want to make the play-offs. Wish moves forward more, so I can feel his chest against my back, then holds up a Tater Tot for me. As if this is all completely normal. As if we've done this a million times before.

Then he looks out the window. The sun is still shining, but it looks like there's a storm approaching. "Hey," he whispers to me, "I'll be back in a sec."

I stand and let him get up, and before I sit down in his seat, I realize something. I'm alone. With his friends. Talk about awkward. I spend the next few minutes pretending to follow the conversation while giving Wish ESP vibes to get his butt back here and save me. He must be in the bathroom.

Five, then ten minutes pass, and I feel my face grow redder and redder as the rest of the people at the table gradually go back to ignoring me. I'm expecting a little alarm to go off and one of them to yell, "Intruder! Intruder!" when the bell rings. I jump up a little too much like I have a rocket in my pants. I turn toward the doors, but Wish is nowhere in sight. Then I catch a glimpse of something large and black outside, half hidden behind the trailers where health and driver's ed are taught. Wish. He's standing out there, staring up at the blinding sun. The storm clouds beyond seem to crowd around his profile, threatening, ominous. Either he's been in sunny L.A. so long that he's fascinated by the thunderstorm, or he's hoping a lightning bolt will strike him down because he sucks at confrontations and doesn't want to deal with the uncomfortable task of breaking up with me. I'm going with Option Two.

16

THE REST OF THE DAY, I field curious glances from people. They look at me as if seeing me for the first time. I'm not sure if they're wondering about the mess of cottage cheese south of my waist or surprised that I sat on a hot guy's lap during lunch period, and not only did he survive, he seemed okay with it. I keep my head down and my mouth shut and manage to make it through the day.

As I'm pulling another monster stack of books from my locker to take home with me, Wish comes up behind me and plants his chin on my shoulder. "Hey, you."

It's so playful and dripping with sweetness that if I'd witnessed any other guy saying it to any other girl, I'd probably have vomited a little in my mouth. When is this charade going to be over? I turn around and face him, still avoiding his eyes. "Hey."

He leans against the locker next to mine, then stretches his arms over his head so that his black shirt lifts and I get a glimpse of a sliver of tan stomach. Oh my goodness. Air. I need air. "So what's going on in that mind of yours?" he asks.

I'm glad it's not obvious, because it's way too embarrassing. The part of my brain that isn't shriveling from oxygen deprivation can only sputter out words like "throbbing" and "juicy" and . . . I need to be neutered. "Um . . ."

"Here's what I'm thinking," he says. "It's been a crazy day. I can see it in your eyes. You're thinking, 'Do I know this guy anymore?' You and me. We haven't had any time to connect."

I gulp. "Connect?"

"Yeah. Alone time." He reaches over and tries to tuck a tuft of my hair, which has somehow left the trapezoid, behind my ear.

My body starts to shiver and twitch as I comprehend what he is saying. Alone time. Alone. As in me and him. Connecting with his throbbing . . .

I jump. "I'm going to miss my bus!" I shout so loudly he jumps, too. My teeth are chattering.

He grins, then holds his hand up in front of my eyes. Something shiny drops from his palm, and he lets it dangle, back and forth, like a hypnotist's chain. A key. A car key. But that's stupid. In Jersey we don't get our licenses until seventeen, not for another whole year.

"You're . . ."

With the other hand, he reaches into his pocket, pulls out his wallet, and flips it open, like a police officer. There's his California driver's license, in one of the sleeves. "Legal," he says.

It strikes me now that he's not just one of the coolest kids in our class. He is right there at the top. The only one with a license. Hell, he's too good for naked cheerleaders.

"Uh . . ."

"I would have driven you this morning if you hadn't blown me off last night," he says, mock hurt in his voice. "So come on. Let's get out of here."

For a second I want to whoop with joy. My busing days are over. Then a cold breeze somehow finds its way under my hairline, making me shiver all down my back. They're not over. He's just . . . not thinking straight. Give him a few days and he'll realize what everyone else at school already knows. And what have I been telling Evie? "Don't get too close. Guys can bite. And by the time they do, you're the one wearing the dog collar."

"Are you sure? I mean, I can just take the bus. Really, it's not a big—"

His cell phone beeps, and he reaches for it. He looks up from the phone and holds a hand out. "No you won't. I insist."

I probably could protest more, but I never did like the bus, and I take one millisecond's look at those piercing blue eyes. Pleading with me. Me. That's all it takes. "Um. Okay."

He helps me lug my books down the hall and out the door, and though the hallway is emptying out, I catch shocked glances from everyone who passes us. Wish doesn't seem to notice. He's checking his phone. He texts something, talking about cross-country tryouts and horrible

Mr. Burns, his chem teacher, and before I know it, we're outside and the sun is shining down on me and all my flaws and I know he's going to turn to me and realize that he's made a horrible mistake. Instead, though, he tilts his face to the sun, as if trying to soak in as many rays as he can. His cell phone beeps again. He grimaces at it and then turns it off. Then, just as I predicted, three steps from the school, he faces me, mouth widening, confusion in his face.

"Earth to Gwen?"

"Um, yeah?"

"You are a million miles away. Did you hear anything I said?"

"No, sorry."

"I asked if your mom still makes the best white cream donuts in the world, and if I could maybe swipe one or a few dozen, if they have any left. I missed them like crazy."

Of course. He's using me to get to my mother's donuts. Now it all makes sense. "We'll have leftovers. She usually makes a whole tray and we don't get many customers in the off-season."

He rubs his hands together as we enter the parking lot. "Cool." We stop next to a silver Ford pickup, and he opens the passenger door for me. He explains that it's a Welcome Back to Jersey gift from his dad. "Surprised the hell out of me," he says. "You know how my dad and I are. But he's the reason I'm here. Said he couldn't stand having a long-distance relationship with his son, so my mom finally agreed to move back."

I raise my eyebrows. His dad is former military, so he's kind of strict and I can't remember ever seeing him smile.

He constantly used to get on Wish for the smallest things: his posture, his haircut, the fact that he'd much rather hang out with me than do a hundred push-ups a day. When his parents split up, I knew right away who he'd choose.

"It's not much, but it's good for carrying surfboards," he explains. Then he lowers his voice an octave: "Makes me feel like a manly man."

I can't help it: I burst out laughing. "You can climb mountainsides. Haul lumber."

"Go to my local NRA meeting. Yeah, all that stuff." He grins, then helps me into the cab of the truck.

If I was in danger of becoming relaxed with him, it doesn't last long. He spends nearly five full minutes adjusting the rearview and side mirrors, and by the time he pulls out of the school parking lot, an uncomfortable silence has already settled in. He fiddles with the controls on his satellite radio, first landing on some hip-hop, then moving to classic rock, then finally stopping on a cheesy pop song. I know he hates that stuff and is just doing it for me. I don't have the heart to tell him that I haven't listened to that kind of stuff since middle school.

I rack my brain, trying to think of something to say, as we cross the bridge over Cellar Bay. Finally, something comes. "How was your first day back?"

He shrugs. "Everything's just about the same."

I nearly choke on the breath I've been holding. The same? I knew that some Hollywood stars were out of touch with reality, but I didn't realize that applied to the entire state of California. "Except your girlfriend," I mumble.

"Huh?"

"It's just . . . Did you ever tell those guys that you were going out with me?"

"Sure. They all know."

"I heard Erica and Terra talking yesterday and they said they thought you were single. They all kind of hate me. So I just feel weird."

"That's because the two of them have a combined IQ of ten. And they don't hate you. They just don't know you. You're quiet. You keep to yourself. You just need me to break the ice, and they'll all love you. Trust me."

"Okay," I say, doubtful, and that's when I notice he's blinking. The sun is bouncing off one of the mirrors, hitting him directly in the eyes. That's got to hurt. I reach over and push his sun visor down. "Better?"

He quickly pushes it back into place, looking alarmed for the first time. For someone as laid-back as Wish, it's weird, and he must sense that, too, because he laughs nervously afterward. "No. I mean, I like the sun. I can see better with it like this, anyway."

"Oh," I say, wondering how that's possible. Maybe the California sun has fried his eyeballs, which would explain why he hasn't noticed how much I've changed. We're pulling up to the bakery, anyway. In another few minutes, I can escape. As soon as he stops at the curb, I push open the door and scoot my backside off the seat. I'm far enough away that even if he was thinking about kissing me, which I know is highly unlikely, it would be completely out of the question.

"Hey," he says, his voice bright. "You up for a walk on the beach? Haven't seen the Atlantic in ages."

I just stare at him. He really wants to spend more time with me? On the beach?

"We can play Gone with the Wind. There's a great breeze. I can whip your butt."

I can't help smiling. So he remembers. When we were little and ignorant, and before we knew who Scarlett O'Hara was, we invented a game called Gone with the Wind. Basically, the only objective of it was to run around as if being lifted up by the breeze, arms out, floating like leaves. Then we would tackle each other, laughing like mad, completely oblivious to everyone staring at us from their beach towels like we had two heads. We'd kick up sand, make a huge disturbance, get the tourists to give us dirty looks and the lifeguards to whistle at us, but we didn't care. We didn't care what anyone thought about us then; it was just fun. That's about it. To this day, I'm not sure how one would win at a game like that.

I cringe as I force away the mental image of him reaching for me, putting his hands on my body, touching the folds of flesh that weren't there all those years ago.

"Maybe some other time. I'm just going to get you those donuts."

I hurry away before he can say another word, and walk into the empty bakery. Christian doesn't even come out when the bell above the door jingles; he's probably OD'd in the back room. I throw a dozen cream donuts into a white paper bag and return to Wish's truck a minute later. "Awesome," he says.

"Yeah." I'm already holding the truck door, ready to slam it. "So, thanks."

"Hey," he says, which makes me turn toward him, and our eyes momentarily meet. He leans over. "Are you sure everything's okay?"

I nod.

"I'll see you tomorrow, then?"

I nod again. "But you don't have to pick me up. I'll just see you at school." When he opens his mouth to protest, I say, "I don't mind taking the bus. I, um, like it."

"Okay," he says, his face solemn. "Have a good—"

I wasn't expecting him to say anything else, so I accidentally slam the door before he can finish. That was rude. I give him a smile and wave and try to look as happy as possible. I'm thinking I pulled it off when I go into the bakery and Christian, who somehow miraculously appeared out of nowhere, says, "Dude, you look like you're coming from your own funeral."

I want to tell him to go blow it out his crack pipe, but I'm still not sure about his past. On the off chance he's a mass murderer, I'd better keep quiet. I'm starving from not eating lunch, so I grab a carton of Nesquik and a coconut strip and walk past him, gnashing my teeth.

"Was that the boyfriend you told me about?" he asks, obviously mistaking my teeth-gnashing for a sign I'm open to conversation.

"I guess. I don't know."

"You don't know?" He laughs. "Because, dude, you guys seem really in love."

I narrow my eyes. Murderer or whatever, he's a jerk and must be silenced. "Could you please not spy on me?"

He shakes his head, those dirty dreads brushing the tops

of his shoulders. "No way, man. You and your sister are the most entertainment I get here."

I give him a look.

He shrugs. "If you don't want me to watch, don't park outside the window."

I definitely prefer the walker-using help of previous years. The most annoying thing about them was the faint smell of approaching death and their tendency to bring up the benefits of Metamucil to customers. "I'm going to start my homework. I know you probably don't know what that is, but . . ."

He's grinning at me like he knows he's under my skin and happy to be there. And I feel the same way I've felt pretty much all day. Foolish.

17

THE NEXT MORNING, I stare up at the ceiling, at a brown-edged water spot in the shape of a boot. Until my mom had the roof fixed, every time it would rain, I'd get the Reilly's Irish Bakery version of Chinese water torture.

But even though I haven't been dripped on in years, I've never felt worse torture in my life.

Wish has always been my best friend. He's never done anything mean to me. He doesn't have that in him. But now he's acting almost too nice. If I could look into his heart, though, I bet I would see the same thing that all my class-mates see when they look at me.

Evie pulls aside the curtain and comes into my room as I'm lying there in the dark. "Are you dead?"

I just groan.

"The bus will be here in fifteen minutes."

95

I roll over. Just thinking about which goofy Hanes sweat-shirt and khaki elastic-waist pants I can wear makes me ill. "I'm not going."

"It's only the first week of school," she says. Then I hear her call, "Ma! Dough is sick."

My mother calls from the kitchen, "What's wrong, hon?"

"I, um, think I had a bad, um, Tater Tot," I say, uttering the first food item that comes to mind. I still can't get the scene of Wish feeding me out of my head. That little potato nugget is forever ingrained in my psyche.

Evie just stands there, shaking her head over me like I'm the result of some horrible science experiment gone wrong. "I would never eat that cafeteria food. If you eat it every day, you'll end up huge. No offense, Dough." In my debilitated state, I somehow manage to muster the energy to smack her really hard on her bony butt. She shouts, "Mo-om!" in her annoying five-year-old tattletale voice, but then Rick's horn blares and she immediately ages ten years before my eyes. "Feel better," she mumbles, running off.

My mom's not the strictest parent in the world. I guess since she dropped out of high school when she was sixteen to marry my dad, she realizes she can't be one to talk. She comes into my room and puts a hand on my forehead, which always calms me. "Well, you just rest, then."

So I spend the entire day in bed. Mostly I just lie there and stare at the boot on the ceiling. I think about reading; there's a copy of *The Hunger Games* on my bedside table, under a layer of dust. I got thirty pages into it on the last day of freshman year and haven't picked it up since. Just looking at the title gives me an appetite. At one point I get up the energy to surf the Internet, which is a mistake, because I land myself on Wish's Facebook page and he has "what's up?" wall messages from everyone and their mother. Literally. A Colleen DeFuca, who must be Fudge's mom, wrote, "So nice to see you last night! Come over for dinner anytime!" As I scroll down the page, I cringe at the dozen or so messages he's gotten in only, like, the last twelve hours, then contemplate ripping the extension cord from the wall and wrapping it around my neck a few times. Then I go back to bed.

At one in the afternoon, though, it hits me: I have school tomorrow. My situation has not improved. And I seriously doubt that the Tater Tot excuse will hold up for another day.

Not only that, since I haven't eaten anything since last night, I'm starving in an eat-my-hand kind of way. Because our fridge is always devoid of everything but fish sticks, I decide to go down and swipe some eats. I'm hoping Christian will be with a customer or so cracked up he doesn't know his ass from his elbow and I can just avoid him. So I tiptoe into the bakery, as ninja-like as a fat girl can, all the while salivating at the thought of a nice buttery onion roll. I'm so focused on the taste of those yummy sweet onions that a full-fledged lioness growl almost escapes when I see Christian sitting there, hunched over a table in the back room, still. Sleeping, I think. His back is to me, but he's blocking the door to the bakery. He's blocking my access to my onion roll, to my bliss. And that makes him evil.

I sidle up behind him. Yes, he must be punished. No, I won't tell my mom that he's dozing on the job, but I'll make him think I'm going to. And then I'll give him a stack of boxes to fold. Oh, yes, I will make him fear me.

When I get closer, his head cocks a bit to the side. So he's not sleeping? Maybe he's doing lines. Then I hear something beneath his chin that sounds strikingly similar to paper rustling . . . a page in a book turning. He's . . . he can't be . . . reading?

I take a few more steps toward him and decide that he must be perusing a manga book or a how-to manual on freebasing. When I'm near enough to peer over his shoulder at the title of the book on the top of the page, I think I must be going blind. It's *The Faerie Queene*. It's Edmund Spenser.

Wait. Crackheads do not read Edmund Spenser. Edmund Spenser is probably the furthest thing from manga I can think of. In fact, I, who am reasonably well read and intelligent, would probably rather read a how-to manual on freebasing than Edmund Spenser.

Suddenly, Christian swings around and faces me. The book and his chair fall to the cracked linoleum. His eyes are huge with surprise. Wait, no, that isn't surprise. He's wearing glasses. Round-lensed spectacles that magnify his eyes into golf balls. For once, he has his dreads pushed back, in a kind of girly white headband, so I can see his eyes. And those goofy glasses. I jump back as he lets out this little piglike squeal. Then he loosens his jaw and whispers, "What the . . . What are you . . ."

I just stand there. Edmund Spenser?

"You scared the crap out of me," he finally says.

"Are you reading that for a class or something?" I ask.

He reaches down and picks it up. "I was just . . ." He looks nervous. He pulls off his glasses and headband and then it's right back to the Christian I've come to expect. "Forget it. Why are you here?"

I sniff loudly, which is pretty stupid, since I'm home because of a stomach thing, but whatever. He doesn't know that. "I'm sick."

With that, I head into the front. I reach into a case and pull out a scrumptious, perfect onion roll, then devour half of it in one bite. When I turn around to search the donut case for some dessert, I see Christian standing in the doorway, watching me. His dreads might shield his eyes from the world, but they don't hide his smug smile.

"What?" Since my mouth is full, it comes out like "Ut?"

"That's bull," he says, coming inside and leaning against the counter. "That dude in the truck . . . your boyfriend. You're avoiding him."

I swallow. "I am not. I'm sick."

He laughs. "Yesterday you couldn't get away from him fast enough, by the looks of it."

"Because I had a lot of homework to do," I say, wondering why I'm having this conversation. I should be upstairs with a gallon of Nesquik and a bag of sugar and *As the World Turns*. "And I was feeling sick."

"Okay," he says doubtfully.

I start to walk away, but then I stop. "I mean, you saw him. Do we . . . I mean, would you ever think that he and I could . . . last?"

Immediately, he shakes his head. "Not a chance." I start to nod in agreement, but then he says, "Not with that look."

"Look?" I act surprised, but I know exactly what he's talking about. The big-Hanes-sweatshirt look.

To my surprise, he points at my face. "That look. Like you're about to die."

I realize that I have such a deep frown and I've been lifting my eyebrows in worry for so long the creases on my forehead must be little canyons. I mentally massage my face so that the corners of my mouth tip up a bit. "I'm not sure what you mean."

"I get it. You're feeling sorry for yourself."

I sigh. "Well, wouldn't you, if your girlfriend transformed into a Victoria's Secret model while you became the Pillsbury Doughboy?"

He shrugs. "If she loved me, why would I care what I looked like?"

Ugh. Guys. So simple. So idiotic. "B-because . . . ," I stammer.

"I'm just saying."

"Thanks, Dr. Phil," I say, stuffing the rest of the roll into my mouth.

"Who you are isn't half as important as who you let others think you are. It's all about perception. And there are ways to make people perceive things that aren't really there."

I cross my arms. "Oh, so you like to let people think you're a pothead loser when you're actually a literary scholar . . . why, again?"

He nods. "If I had come in here all clean-cut and raring to go, your mother would have given me a shitload of things to do. As it was, you guys wanted to get as far away from me as possible, as quickly as possible."

My jaw drops. "You mean, it really is all an act?"

He smiles. "It's not just acting lessons and airbrushing that makes us drool over Hollywood stars. There are a lot of techniques for enhancing one's star qualities. My mom's an actress, so she should know."

No, your mom's a prostitute, I think, but I'm too intrigued by this theory to correct him. He's got to be kidding, right? "That is so warped."

"How is it, if it helps you?" He says that very philosophically, as if he's reciting the Tao of Christian or something.

I want to smack that smug look off his face. "You didn't really fool me. That whole 'May I have a cupcake?' thing was not very scary. Very Oliver Twist."

He waves me off. "What are you talking about? You almost pissed yourself when I got in your space. I bet you ran upstairs and asked your mom what prison I'd just been released from."

I keep my mouth shut.

"Speaking of Mom, Grams said she gave you all her leftover clothes. So why are you wearing stuff like"—he points to my raggy sweatpants—"that?"

"Excuse me, I didn't know I had to dress in a prom gown to be sick," I mutter. "It was very nice of Melinda, but tight snakeskin minidresses don't exactly work for me."

He squints at me. "Oh, right. Mom was here doing a play called *Toots* back then. It was about a stripper. She got an award for that."

I swallow. "You mean, she doesn't . . ."

"Always dress like that? No," he says as if I'm an idiot. "She's always getting clothes sent to her from all these designers."

"Really?" I suddenly have an uncontrollable urge to go through that bag. Four minutes after she'd presented it to me, it was stuffed behind my hamper, where dust bunnies go to die.

"Did you think my mom was really a stripper?"

Well, no, actually, I'd thought a lot worse, but I shan't be telling him that. I'm struggling to think of a believable lie when he grins.

"That's good. She's an actress. It's her job to fool you."

"It worked," I admit. "But she's the actress. You're just a guy working at a bakery. Why do you do it?"

He shrugs. "Why the hell not? I'm not hurting anyone this way."

"But . . . aren't people disappointed when they find out that's not really you?"

"It's all me. I'm not just one flavor. You're not, either. So it all comes down to which 'you' you want to show the world." He thinks for a moment. "I used to do a lot of crazy . . . Well, forget it."

There's something he's thinking of saying, but I'm too busy trying to digest this new concept to pay attention. Which "me" do I want to show the world? Sure, I guess I could try to switch it up a little, show off the more confident, unreserved me, the me I save for singing in the shower and goofing off at home, instead of the dorky me that seems to want to show itself far more often. But would that version of me come out? Maybe if I mentally pushed myself, it would. Maybe my confident flavor would ooze through. Flavor. I need another donut. I grab a glazed ring off the shelf and start to lick the icing off it. "Are you really reading Edmund Spenser for fun?"

He starts to answer, just as the bell above the door jingles. Two white-haired ladies hobble in, and I take that as a cue to run upstairs and check out the bag of clothes Melinda gave me. In my room, I reach behind my hamper and pull out the shopping bag. It's stuffed to the top, and for the first time I realize that none of the fabric poking out resembles snakeskin, or anything tacky, at all. I dump the bag out on my mattress and inspect some of the pieces. They don't have tags on them, but I can already tell they make the nicest thing in my closet, the frilly church-lady blouse that was ruined by blood yesterday, look like an XXL Hanes sweatshirt.

I fluff out a sheer pink dress and hold it against my body, imagining myself with Wish at homecoming. In that dress, I'd almost look like I belonged with him.

I stand in front of the mirror and do a twirl. "What flavor are you?" I murmur, and then I realize that I am talking to myself, and that while designer clothes might be able to hide my butt, they probably won't be able to hide that I am going nuts.

18

I SPEND THE REST of the day rushing around the apartment like a madwoman, confiscating things from Evie's room, rifling through my mom's makeup bag, and spontaneously breaking into jumping jack binges from the adrenaline. Every time my arms meet over my head, I grunt out, "What flavor are you?" like a drill sergeant. "I am too hot for Erica Dunleavy. Way too hot for Terra Goldbar. Rick Rothman has nothing on me!" I chant until I'm out of breath.

While I'm lying on the floor of the living area, recovering, Evie and my mom come in. My mom's eyes widen. "Oh! Did you faint?"

"Um, no," I say, struggling to sit up.

Evie says nothing until she spots a pile of her things on

one of the chairs. "What are you doing with my stuff?" she demands.

"Just borrowing."

"Oh, okay," she says, shrugging. She drops her bag and inspects the pile. "You're going to curl your hair? And wear eyeliner?"

I shrug.

"Aw, it's for Wish, isn't it? That's cute," she says, like I'm in preschool.

"No, it's for a science experiment," I mutter.

She nods, then scrunches her nose in confusion. I can tell she's wondering why all they do in Intro to Physical Science is fire up Bunsen burners. When her eyes light up, I know she's thinking about the possibility of getting an A in science junior year, for the first time ever, if makeovers are on the syllabus. "Do you want help?" she asks.

I've never used a curling iron before, and I'll probably burn my forehead to a crisp, but I shake my head. I need to focus, and I doubt I'll be able to with Evie popping her gum and, well, just existing.

First I start with a shower. I shave and loofah myself until my skin glows red. As I'm applying some of Evie's self-tanner, my mother bangs on the bathroom door.

"Indecent!" I shout.

"Dinner!" she shouts back. I don't smell anything like fish sticks, so it must be french-bread pizza night.

"Not hungry," I answer. I'm too busy chanting my mantra to think about eating. *You are strong. You are beautiful. Wish is lucky to have you.*

When I'm done, I sit on the toilet lid, naked, waiting for my body to dry. I hope I'm not all streaky. While I wait, I read an article in one of Evie's *Seventeen* magazines about how to tweeze eyebrows. It sounds painful and dangerous, but my chanting must be working, because I find the confidence to attempt it. I use an emery board to draw an imaginary line across my brow, just like the article instructs, which sounds kind of stupid, but it works. When I'm done, I stand back and look at myself. Wow. Estee Lauder would approve.

Next I do a manicure and a pedicure. The polish gets everywhere but on my nails at first, but eventually, with the help of cotton swabs and a gallon of remover, I do a passable job.

Soon Evie's banging on the door. "I have to pee," she grumbles. "Oh, and Wish is on the phone."

With the swami towel insulating my ears, I didn't hear the phone ring. I put on my robe and waddle into the kitchen as fast as my feet, with little toe separators intact, will carry me. "Hello?"

"Hey, you."

Wish's voice is soft, scrumptious. It makes me want to sputter, "I'm not worthy!" into the receiver, but I bite my tongue and think, What would be the fun and sexy thing to say? "Hi, baby," escapes.

Oh, God. That does not sound like me. I don't even sound PG-13 rated. I sound like Toots, the old fat stripper Christian's mom played.

There's a pause. "Have you been drinking?"

I suck in a breath. "No, why?" I can sound fun and sexy

without sounding like a stripper. Happy medium. Like Erica Dunleavy. Channel Erica Dunleavy, Dough. You can do it. "Have you?"

I let out this giggle that sounds like I have been not only drinking, but sucking helium and popping Valium as well. Stop it, stop it, stop it! Get control. You can do this.

Wish ignores the question. "Evie told me you were sick. Are you feeling better?" he asks. That's when I realize I should probably be acting like a recovering sick person, instead of a phone sex girl.

I muster a cough, which is just as silly as my sniff in front of Christian. Thanks to Evie's vagueness, she probably didn't tell him my bad Tater Tot excuse. "Much better," I say, chanting, Confident, confident, confident! in my head. It works. I don't sound squeaky at all. "How are you?"

"Good. I missed you."

I'm about to say, "Why, do I owe you money?" But I stop myself. "Aw, you're sweet."

"So, you coming to school tomorrow?"

"Yeah." I take a deep breath and say, "Can I ask you a favor? Would you mind driving me?"

Another pause. "Now, Gwen, you know I wouldn't," he says in his "silly you" tone. "I'll be there at seven. Cool?"

"Fantastic!" I say with so much enthusiasm you'd think I just got a free trip to Disney. I am such a fraud. No, no, I am confident. I am beautiful.

"Great. See you then," he says.

I hang up the phone, turn, and see my mother and Evie staring at me. They both have their forks suspended midway between their plates and their mouths. A big clump of mac and cheese falls off my mother's, right into her lap. "Sugar!" she cries. Then she swabs her pants with a napkin and says, "Why are you all red?"

Evie points at my pedicure, my delicate pink toenails, all grinning up at me. "Pretty," she says.

I can't help smiling. I don't think anything of mine, even my feet, has been called that in a very long time.

19

I SET MY ALARM CLOCK for three-thirty in the morning, which is ridiculously early for school, but no earlier than I've been waking up every day to help with the bakery. There's still more to do, and I want to be prepared. The first thing I do is switch on the light and inspect my skin. No self-tanner streaks. Thank the fake-sun gods.

My mother's heading out the door in her baker's whites when I walk into the kitchen. "Are you feeling all right, hon?" she asks.

"Yeah, I'm—"

"Your stomach's okay?"

"Yeah, I'm just going to work out a little," I say, pointing to the television.

I read in a magazine once that exercise boosts confidence. It releases endorphins, which is the equivalent of three glasses of wine. Since I need all the help I can get, I spend an hour kicking and jabbing, until I'm drenched in sweat. An hour of Tae Bo, coupled with not eating dinner or snacks the night before, and the only thing that feels lighter is my head.

Still, I make it into the shower without passing out and then spend an hour trying to curl my hair into nice, loose, flowy curls that don't particularly look like any geometric shape. Then I apply all the makeup I laid out last night: mascara, eyeliner, blush, lip gloss. Then I pull on a pair of black capris and a really cute black top covered with white, yellow, and blue daisies. I throw on my black flip-flops and tousle and spray my hair again, and two hours after I started, I'm done.

Evie's just coming out of her room, tossing her hair into a clip, when she spots me. "Oh" is all she says at first.

"Is that oh, good, or oh, yuck?"

"No, it's . . ." She sniffs, overcome with emotion. She bounds over to me and touches my shirt, maybe to make sure I'm real. "Wow. Where did you get this?"

"Melinda's daughter. She left all these clothes—"

"The prostitute?"

I'm about to tell her that it's a long story when a car horn blares. Evie turns and bounces toward the window. She opens the slats and peeks through. "It's Wish," she says.

"You need a ride?" I ask.

"Oh." She thinks for a moment, then waves me off. "No, that's okay. It would probably be too crowded with Becca and me. Besides, I really think everything with you and Rick was just a misunderstanding. I mean—"

I grab my bag and put up my hand. "Fine. Gotta go."

Taking a breath, I head outside. It's a nice day; the sun is already warm and the birds are singing like crazy. When I step down the last stair on the rickety staircase on the side of the building, Wish's truck comes into view. He's standing on the curb, ready to open the passenger-side door, like a real gentleman. He takes one look at me and blinks. "Whoa. I'd say you're feeling better."

"Much." I grin. I think about doing a little twirl to show off my stuff, but I decide I will probably trip and end up bleeding on the sidewalk. "Do you like?"

"Very much. You did your hair, right?" He reaches out and twists a curl around his finger.

"Um, yeah." Well, at least he recognized that, even if he didn't notice the thirty other things I did. I've heard men aren't the most observant when it comes to that.

I climb into his truck. Again, I notice he has the mirrors tilted so that the sun is streaming into his eyes, making them look like pools of chlorinated water. To ward off any more uncomfortable silences, I thought of topics of conversation during most of the two hours I spent getting ready. Nothing heavy, just light, fun things. As he takes off toward the bridge, I see Rick's BMW in the rearview mirror and pull one out of my arsenal. "So, how are the waves here compared to the ones in California?"

Wish doesn't answer me. It was a good question, or at least I thought it was. Not too difficult, and it shows I care about his hobbies. In fact, it was at the top of my list of "safe" topics to talk about. Topics like bodily functions, sex, and body parts normally hidden by clothing were on my "extremely unsafe" list, but surfing, well, I figured that to be pretty harmless. Until now.

I realize he's staring out the rearview mirror, too, at my sister as she hops into Rick's convertible. "He's not driving your sister to school, is he?"

"Who? Rick? Yeah." I roll my eyes. "She says she's infatuated with his car only, but I don't buy it."

He swings the truck into third gear, and I marvel at how manly his hairy forearm looks on the stick. I'm just deciding that there is nothing sexier than a guy shifting a manual transmission when he says, "If I had a sister, I'd never let her anywhere near that guy."

"Believe me, I've warned her. It didn't do any good."

He pauses. "I know you did. But she's not listening, because you're too nice." He thinks for a second. "Maybe I should talk to her."

"Be my guest."

"Kids these days . . ." He puts on his best old-fogey voice and pumps his fist in the air. "I feel sorry for her."

"What for?"

He sighs. "Being beautiful. It's not fun. People want things from you. They suck you dry." He gives me a half smile. "So I hear."

So he has noticed Evie's beauty, even though he hasn't noticed my lack thereof. He's obviously speaking from personal experience. I can't add anything to the conversation, so I just shrug.

"You're too nice. I would scream at her to stay away. I would smack it into her," he says.

"Sure you would." The thing is, even though he's calling

me nice, he's the one who should be applying for sainthood. He hardly knows Evie, yet he doesn't want to see her hurt. And here I am, related by blood to Evie and actually a little excited to see Rick teach her a lesson so I can say, "I told you so." In fact, I get a small thrill thinking about it. "You think Rick is going to break her heart?" I ask as we sail over the bridge to the mainland. The windows are open, letting in the cool bay breeze, and seagulls are perched on every streetlight, almost like an audience, wondering what stupid question I'll ask next.

"I think he's going to show his bad side to her, sooner or later. It always comes through, eventually, but the sooner it does, the better off she'll be."

"He already did show his bad side," I say, thinking about that day in the bakery. "She seems immune."

He raises his eyebrows. "Really?"

"She's never really dated anyone before," I explain, kind of embarrassed, since I'm not Miss Experience myself. "She's only fourteen. It's all new to her."

I don't bother to add that it's all new to me, too. He doesn't have to be Einstein to know that, anyway.

We pull into the school's driveway, and I'm happy I still have almost my entire arsenal of conversation topics intact. Wish and I didn't have a pause in conversation at all, and I never once felt like I wanted to throw up. Things are going great.

But right then, Wish downshifts to second, then reaches over and puts his hand on my knee. Before I can tell my mouth to behave, I let out a little scream.

He snatches his hand away. "Oops."

I want to say something smooth, like "Hot hands," since he did practically burn me the last time with his finger, it was so warm. Or was that just my nutty imagination? But I'm wearing pants, so I have no idea what temperature his hand is. It was just a nice, friendly gesture, something a parent would do to a child, or a teacher would do to a student, Dough. It did not warrant a scream or a shriek or anything of the sort. Moron. "It just . . . surprised me," I say, wooden. "You can do it again."

He doesn't bother. I don't blame him. The invitation was like "Oh yes, please stick needles in my eyeballs." He just slides into a parking space in the junior lot and looks at me. "I know, I know. We can take things slow," he says, reading my mind. He pats my cheek gently, the heat from his hand radiating over my face, making it burn again. Ouch. He gives the word "hottie" a whole new meaning.

I smile shyly, realizing that no girl in her right mind, Erica or anyone, would need to take it slow. Not with a guy like Wish. She would have jumped on him by now. Ravished his body, stuffed a house key and a slip of paper with her phone number into his pants. I want to grab his hand and put it back on my knee, but that's when I notice that though it's again over eighty degrees, he's wearing the same black shirt he wore yesterday. Or maybe a different one, but it looks the same. For a guy who just came from California, isn't that weird?

I kind of like it. It's nice that there's one weird thing about Wish, as it makes the hundreds of weird things about me seem slightly less apparent.

Just slightly.

Cleansing breaths. In. Out. In. Out.

As we get closer to the crowd of students waiting outside for the first bell to ring, it occurs to me that I don't look normal. Rather, I look like I'm in labor or doing a stair climb of the Empire State Building. I try to hide it by breathing through my nose, but I know that my nostrils are probably flaring like two big black holes, and then my chest hurts and I begin to feel dizzy. Oxygen. I need more oxygen.

Before I can go looking for a mask and tank, we somehow end up in the crowd. I'm only slightly aware that I'm trailing behind Wish, like some ugly boil on his backside, instead of walking beside him, like his equal. In an echo chamber, to my own heartbeat, I hear someone call, "Wish, yo, Wish!" and Wish turns and starts to head there, so I follow. This time, I'm positive I look like a butt boil. When Wish stops, I nearly step on the heels of his Vans and smack my nose between his shoulder blades. I take a step to the side and the same crowd from Wednesday's lunch table's there, in a tight U, open just enough so that Wish can fill the space and make it a circle.

Confidence, I tell myself, quickly attaching myself to Wish's side before the circle can close. The guy on my right, Skull, elbows me in the boobs. It only hurts like hell for a second.

I don't think he recognizes me at first, but then he gives me a nod. "Word."

I'm not sure why, but I take it as an apology. "It's okay!" I burst out really loudly, grabbing his massive, muscle-bound arm and squeezing it a little. I never knew this, but the Confident Me likes to touch people. A lot. It doesn't cross my mind that Skull might be one of those people who hate being fondled by strangers until I catch him looking at my hand, on his arm, with dark, murderous eyes. Slowly, I release my grip, and it becomes obvious to me that all eyes in the group are on me.

"Oh, hey, all!" I say, giving a big wave. Again, I'm loud enough for residents of China to hear. Terra's standing across from me, biting her lip in a rare speechless moment. "Wow, fantastic . . ." My eyes trail down her body as I look for something to compliment. What? Blouse, jeans, shoes. What? They're all pretty fantastic. I can take my pick. Nails. Bag. No, nails. Wait, bag. I finally spit out, "Nag."

She stares at me. Destiny snorts, then looks at Erica. "Did she just call her a fantastic nag?"

"I mean, bag," I say more softly so the entire continent can't hear me this time. I move into the center of the circle, which I think might be against their Laws of Social Interaction, from the way they're all staring at me, open-jawed. But Confident Me makes her own rules. I start to touch the rough fabric. There I go again, Miss Happy Fingers, fondling everything that doesn't belong to me. "What is it?"

She gives me a look, and I know she's on to me. The Hanes wardrobe I've sported over the past four years might have given her the tip-off that I'm not exactly a member of the Versace family. She says a name, something obviously foreign, probably spelled with a bunch of accents and squiggles and silent letters.

It must be a big deal, because Destiny raises her eyebrows, and suddenly, even she can't keep her hands off the bag. "Seriously? Love it."

It's freaking burlap. But I don't bother to mention that it looks like something horses would eat out of. After all, I've already called Terra a nag. Considering her unfortunate resemblance, it's best to avoid any more horse associations for the rest of . . . well, for the rest of forever.

"Trés chic," I find myself saying. What the . . . I don't speak French. But Confident Me can speak in many tongues, I guess. I might have gotten that from an episode of *Project Runway*.

Strangely, none of them thinks it sounds as pretentious as I do. Erica looks me over, and right when I'm sure she's about to point out my rolls of flesh, she says, "Speaking of chic, nice top. It's Marc, isn't it?"

Oh my God. Erica the Amazing just complimented me. Me! I fish for the sarcasm in her voice, but there is none. She's genuinely admiring my blouse. But who is Marc? Marc, Marc, Marc. I think there was a kid in our class in second grade named Marc, but he moved away. I look over my shoulder to see if he's somehow magically reinserted himself into the circle, but there's no one new there, just Skull and Wish, discussing something sports related again.

The confusion on my face must be a glowing beacon, because she says, "Jacobs? The designer?"

"Oh. Yes." Obviously it's not but I can't stop my head from nodding like it's on a puppet string. I can't even tell you my own name right now.

Destiny's eyes narrow. "I didn't know Marc made things that size."

Terra snorts. But Erica waves her off. "Stop it, Des," she says, moving closer to me. "It's really nice. Brings out the color in your eyes."

My heart starts to twitter. She has seen past my designer shirt, to my eyes. To me. And not the part of me that's immediately obvious, either. I have to fight the momentary compulsion to leap into her arms. "Thanks," I gush.

Then silence. Crap.

"So," I say, making the word really long and loud, mentally sorting through the topics of conversation I planned. I'm on her radar. This is my moment. I have to pounce on it now, before I become invisible again. "You guys going to the party tonight?"

Terra laughs. "Well. I guess I should. Since it's at my house."

"Oh. Right," I say as Destiny giggles into her fist. I point at her and Erica. "I meant these guys."

Erica nods. "We'll be there. You?"

I nod back, maybe a little too eagerly. "Oh, yeah. I need to wind down. It's been a tough week."

Destiny grins wickedly at Terra. "Great. You'll have to do some of the Goldbar family's famous Jell-O shots."

Terra nods in agreement.

I swallow. Not only do I not particularly like Jell-O or any food that bears such a striking resemblance to my butt, I've never had a drink in my life. Ever. Not even a taste of champagne at a family wedding. And I've never really felt the desire to have one, either. "Okay," I say, as brightly as possible.

"What are you wearing?" Terra asks Destiny, and Destiny

launches into this long-winded description of every piece of merchandise that will be on her body, filled with many more foreign names with squiggles and accents. Terra then does her rundown. I make a mental note that everyone is going to be wearing sundresses, and pray I have something suitable in Melinda's magic bag.

"What about you?" Destiny asks me. The snootiness hasn't disappeared from her voice.

I'm about to say I'm still thinking about it when Erica chimes in, "You can just wear what you have on. It's hot."

A hand appears on my shoulder. It's Wish. I'd somehow, in my lovefest with Erica, forgotten all about him. But Destiny hasn't. She gives him a smoldering look and then catches sight of his hand on me and shakes her head in dismay. "Would you ladies like to begin another day of learning?" he says, bowing and directing us to the front door.

They all giggle at him. He hooks his arm through mine, and I don't have to worry about trailing behind him. For the first time that day, I almost feel safe.

20

IN HOMEROOM, I expect things to deteriorate quickly. I expect Terra and Erica and Destiny to ignore me. Destiny turns her back on me and starts to inspect a lock of her platinum mane for split ends, but Erica offers me a stick of gum. It's a new, funky passion fruit–smoothie flavor that only cool people like Erica would possess. I take it like it's a bar of gold and for a second think about preserving the wrapper in my diary. Terra must have decided that since Erica finds me suitable enough to share her gum with, I'm worthy of conversation. She starts snapping her gum and talking faster than an auctioneer.

"So, like, you're friends with Wish, huh? He's my cousin. Did you know? Well, he is. He's, like, a really cool guy. How long have you known him?"

It's thrilling and dizzying at once. These girls are

buzzing around me, asking me questions about Wish, like I matter. But they're acting like I just appeared out of nowhere. Like I haven't been sitting in class with them for the past four years. It's like I've been wearing an invisibility cloak. I say to myself, No, it's because they're so busy doing Jell-O shots or texting messages to each other or whatever they do that it's only momentary forgetfulness. They have to realize I've been in classes with them all these years, even if they did ignore me, right? I'm about to answer, "Hello? I've known him since first grade?" when Erica speaks. She leans over and says, "So, did you move here from California, too?"

Unbelievable.

Okay, there are over fifteen hundred kids in the school, and since I've always been in the advanced curriculum, I haven't shared a lot of classes with these girls. Erica has school-wide fame for the sex-kitten thing she has going on, and though she'll never be a Rhodes scholar, I thought that having the occasional homeroom or lunch with her meant I was at least on her radar. And I always assumed that Terra knew I had some connection to Wish, because they're cousins. She must; she's thrown enough icy glares my way to freeze the equator. She'll straighten Erica out.

Right now.

Okay, now.

Instead, Terra looks expectantly at me, waiting for an answer.

My mouth opens, but nothing comes out, so I look like part of a bad ventriloquist act. "No, I . . . ," I begin. What do I say? I'm the doofus who sat behind you the past few years, and you just never noticed because I was too doofy to breathe your air? I swallow. "Um. Uh. Yeah."

"Cool, L.A.?" Terra asks, oblivious to my mouth, which is hanging open wide enough to swallow her head.

"Um." I turn and look at Destiny. She's suddenly interested in the conversation again.

She drops her hair over her shoulder and gives her head a shake, like she's the lost child of the Pantene family, and her lips curl over her teeth. "I thought everyone in Southern California was thin," she drawls.

"Um . . . ," I begin, emotions flooding me so quickly that I can't even bother to be insulted by Destiny's fat comment. I'm well insulated against fat comments, I guess. The only things going through my mind are that 1) none of these girls realize I have been part of their class since the beginning of junior high, and 2) this is the absolute best thing that has ever happened to me.

I mean, before Wish, I wasn't just a random nobody that everyone detested. No! I have no history at Cellar Bay. I could have partied with Britney and Paris in L.A. for all they know. I could be George Clooney's love child. No past embarrassments, like the time I threw up on my teacher's head or the time I wore white pants over my hot pink Tuesday undies. Nothing! I am free!

"We've been dating for a few years," I say vaguely, still not convinced that they won't suddenly go, "Hey, waaaait, I remember you. . . ."

Erica leans in. "Seriously? So tell me. Wish must be really good, right?"

I gulp. Yeah, sure he's good, but that's probably not the way she means it.

"Ew," Terra gasps, and stuffs her fingers in her ears, preschool-like. "I am so not listening to this. He's my cousin."

Erica seems to enjoy making Terra squirm. "He has such fantastic lips. He's a great kisser, right?"

Destiny narrows her eyes. "Have you done it with him?" She looks at Erica. "I think she's still a virgin."

What about all color draining from my face screams "virgin"? I wonder.

Erica crosses her arms and addresses Destiny like she's a mental patient who's just been caught wearing her pants on her head again. "She said they've been going out for a few years. You do not go out with someone for that long and not do it with them."

There it is, the Erica Proclamation. Sex must happen if you date a person for a few years, and if not, you are obviously a candidate for hanging from the neck until dead. As she says it, trumpets sound. I half expect a little scribe to come by with a very official parchment scroll and take down every last word. So let it be written, so let it be done. It's strange; I thought that to win the undivided attention of these three, I'd have to, I don't know, gnaw off my own foot or something. I didn't realize all I'd have to do is make up a sex life with Wish.

The room gets a little fuzzy, but I recover and choke out, "Oh, of course we have." My mind says stop, but for some reason my mouth keeps going. "I thought you meant . . . um, like, was he good with charity work or something."

So even though I supposedly do Wish, which should make me a rock star, I still cannot shake the cloud of lameness that follows me. Luckily, they don't seem to notice. Erica raises her eyebrows. "So he is good?"

This is the weirdest conversation I've ever had. It's like trying to converse with three extraterrestrials. Even if I'd had sex with Wish, I wouldn't have anything to compare him to. But then again, this is the new Gwendolyn Reilly. New clothes, new hair, new past, new sexual history. "Yeah," I say. "Really good."

"I knew it." Erica grins her little sex-kitten grin again and pulls out a small notebook. "Wish always comes out on top."

Terra still has her fingers in her ears and is singing "Do-Re-Mi" to herself. Destiny rolls her eyes and says, "Everyone knows how Erica likes it on top."

Erica shrugs. "It's just better that way." Then she looks at me. "Don't you think so, Gwen?"

I nod ferociously, hoping we can change the subject before they realize that my being on top of anything is the quickest way to turn it into a pancake. "Oh. Yeah."

"He has the nicest ass, too. You must just want to squeeze it all the time." She makes a motion like she's squeezing produce for freshness. I peer over at the notebook as she turns the pages. "Hottest. Sweetest. Nicest body. Most athletic." She grins at me. "Your boyfriend is at the top of all of them. Well, not best dressed and nicest car. But everything else."

"Really?" I can't say anything else. I guess I'm waiting

for one of them to pipe in with "But you, on the other hand . . ." But it never comes.

"Ever since he's moved back, he's been our Would You Rather champion," Erica says instead.

"Champion?" I ask. I never thought there was any way to win at Would You Rather. Wish and I used to play it all the time. Eat someone else's fingernail or walk fifty miles? Go to school naked or eat someone's puke?

Terra sighs. "Not with me." She looks at me and explains. "Would You Rather is where one person names two people, and you have to say which one you'd rather sleep with. Wish always wins."

I should have known they'd find a way to turn even the most innocuous memory of my childhood into something sex-related. I bet when they play Monopoly, they pretend the little red hotels are brothels.

"He wins out over all the guys in school. Most of Hollywood, too," Erica says.

I feel the banana I ate for breakfast trying to force its way up my throat. So Erica and Destiny would rather spend a night with Wish than with, say, a gazillionaire Hollywood actor that millions of teenage girls lust after on a nightly basis. And yet nobody's looking at me and thinking there's something wrong with me and Wish together. Well, maybe they are, but they're not saying it.

"So, is his ass really as perfect out of those jeans as it is in them?" Erica asks, pressing me.

I don't answer. I don't know how to. I just smile dumbly. I'm not sure if I'm feeling uncomfortable because I don't know (or care to know) the answer to that question right now, or because I've watched enough soap operas to know that girls like Erica don't let a measly thing like a girlfriend stand in the way of getting what they want. And Erica obviously wants to treat my boyfriend's backside like a cantaloupe.

"You must squeeze it constantly. I mean, how can you not want to squeeze that ass of his constantly?"

I shrug. "Um, I'm not really an ass girl," I say, which is true. I read in *Cosmo* or *Glamour* that some guys are boob men, while other guys like legs. At the time, I wondered how hard it would be to find a guy who was a beer-gut man. Anyway, it must be the same for girls, right? There's nothing wrong with not being an ass girl.

"Oh, you should just squeeze it a little, every day. I would." Erica gives me a little playful pinch on the elbow. I jump, because I'm not expecting it, since people like Erica strike me as the type who would sooner touch doggie doo than unimportant people like me. "So, tell us more."

I fight the overwhelming urge to run for the door. I'm still not convinced that this conversation—this day—can be happening to me. Maybe a little part of each of their brains did remember the goober Dough but then decided that it was a mathematical impossibility for the butt of all their jokes of previous years to be involved with Wish. So to deal with this new and impossible information, their brains simply created a new me. It's a psychological coping mechanism. I hear the words of encouragement Christian gave me: Act confident until you are confident. I remember thinking that that philosophy was crazy, that people would see through it quicker than through cellophane.

Now he sounds like a genius.

So I put on my biggest, most confident smile, say, "What would you like to know?" and hope that Wish doesn't find out about this conversation while I'm alive. Considering how fast my heart is beating, that might not be for long.

21

THE REST OF THE MORNING, two girls offer to share their notes with me, three tell me they love my outfit, and some dude picks up my pen for me when I accidentally drop it. This is a big step up from my previous status, which was the human equivalent of packing peanuts and three a.m. infomercials. You know, just taking up space.

Before I know it, it's lunch. Time to see Wish again. As I navigate away from my locker, I see a row of couples engaged in PDA. This isn't something I noticed before, maybe because I steered clear of that stuff. Now I can't stop looking. Something tells me that if Erica were going out with Wish, she'd be all over him. Maybe I should run up to him and surprise him with a big first wet one, the stuff of movie legends, so romantic and heart-stopping that he pulls away from me, breathless, and says, "Wow. Gwen, never leave me."

Instead, the first thing I do when I see him, standing at the A-list table with his Phillies cap on backward and a french fry crammed between his lips like a cigarette, is blush. Then he turns and notices me, and a slow smile spreads on his face as he sucks the last of the fry into his mouth. Somehow he manages to do this and still look sexy. So the heat on my cheeks, which was mild before, gets cranked up so high that I think steam starts coming off them. Everything in my line of vision gets fuzzy.

It's not like I didn't know he was beautiful and hot and something that the girls would go crazy for. But now that I've seen him topping every one of Erica's lists, the whole "acting confident until you are" I've been trying to do seems pretty freaking impossible. It's one thing to talk sex with Erica and the girls, but another thing entirely to perform. If I ran up to kiss him, we'd most likely end up bonking heads.

"Hey," he says as I near him. "You want something up at the line? My treat."

Food is the last thing on my mind, obviously, because I can't get the conversation with the girls out of my head. What, exactly, makes Wish's butt the object of such enthu-siasm? He's half turned toward me, so I have to crane my neck at a rather unnatural angle to see it, and then, suddenly—

"Hello?" My eyes trail upward, to Wish's questioning face. "What are you doing?"

I shrug, innocent.

"Want something at the line?"

I shake my head, and I see Erica throw her books down on the table beside me. I wonder what she would do at a moment like this, but it doesn't take long to know the answer. Wish starts digging into his pockets for change. He's close to me, thus so is his backside. Now would be the perfect time to do it. Now. Right now. And it's like I can't control myself. As if I'm having an out-of-body experience, I see my hand, shaped like a crab claw, going in for the kill. . . .

"Whoa!" Wish jumps and stares at me, clearly astonished. As do half the people in the cafeteria.

"Um. Hurry back, now," I say, giving him my most seductive, pouty gaze, which I think probably looks like I pressed my face up against a window, from the way he recoils in horror. Okay, totally not the reaction I was aiming for.

Instead of going up to the line, he walks over to the windows. "Is it supposed to rain today?"

The day started out brilliantly sunny, but now clouds are moving in. And it doesn't just look like an afternoon thunderstorm, which are common during hot days in Jersey. It looks like we're in for a good dousing. "Um, I think. But it's supposed to end by early evening."

He nods thoughtfully. "Okay," he says, then heads off toward the line.

I can still feel the denim of his jeans and the firm flesh beneath them on my fingertips. Nice, I guess, but I don't really have anything to compare it to. I have to clasp my other hand over my fingers to keep them from trembling. When I look up at Erica, she's giving me a satisfied smile. Like she's proud of me.

22

WHEN SCHOOL ENDS, I expect Wish to show up at my locker, wielding the keys to his truck and nipping at my heels like a puppy. Since I've acted totally outside my comfort zone all day, I can't wait to get home. I spend a few minutes straightening my locker, but he doesn't come. I peer down the hallway and finally see him trudging toward me, head down. "Hi," I say to him, as brightly as possible.

Maybe it's just that the rain has been falling and the hallway is dark, but his eyes look black-rimmed, troubled. "Hey."

Okay, wait. When I wanted to run in the other direction, he was practically all over me. Now that I'm being all friendly, he's the one running away? Guys can bite. And by the time they do, you're the one wearing the dog collar. "Everything okay?" I ask, trying to sound nonchalant, even though my palms are sweating.

He nods. "Yeah. Ready?" he says, as if there's an appointment he's late for. He doesn't bother to look at me, just continues cruising down the hallway. I follow at his heels, like his butt boil again.

Well, I think as we head off toward the parking lot, I knew this was bound to happen eventually. Even a wardrobe designed by Marc What's-his-face couldn't postpone the inevitable. If I'm lucky, he'll break things off before the party tonight, and I can spend my Friday in bed with Ben & Jerry instead of stressing over whether anyone can see the mongo zit I felt blossoming on my chin last period.

When we get outside, the storm has dissolved to a drizzle. Wish bites his tongue and stares at the clouds. "You said clear skies tonight?"

I nod, wondering why the intense interest in the weather. It's not like Terra's party is outside or anything.

Still the gentleman, he pulls me to his side and tents his big nylon jacket over us. I try not to pay attention to the spicy smell of his aftershave or the hard curve of his ribs brushing against my fleshy arm . . . but of course, trying not to pay attention means that that's all I pay attention to, so I nearly trip on the curb when we get to his truck. And then, on the ride home, he's quiet. I keep waiting for him to open up his mouth and for "It's just not working . . ." to break the silence. Instead, he just sits there, rubbing his shoulder blade every once in a while.

When we pull up to the bakery, he turns to me, still rubbing his shoulder, and I think, This is it. But he says, "So, is nine okay?"

I sit there, speechless, perched on the edge of his leather

seat, which I'd heretofore been expecting my backside never to come in contact with again. Nine. Nine what? Nine is a perfectly okay number, I guess.

He must see my brain working overtime. "To pick you up? For the party?"

I exhale so deeply I bet he can smell on my breath the one Dorito I allowed myself to eat at lunch today. "Uh, yeah."

He looks at the ground. "Hey, listen, I wanted to talk to you about something."

"I know," I say. The moment I've been waiting for. "I know what it is."

"You don't have to do that," he says. "Okay?"

I squint at him. "Do what?"

"Act like those girls, or whatever. Just be Gwen. Be you. All right?"

My face burns when I realize what he's talking about. Someone must have let him in on the sex conversation. Or maybe he's talking about the disastrous Operation Butt Grab. "Uh. Okay," I say. I scramble out of his truck in a daze, barely feeling the raindrops as they fall on me. I can't help thinking that Wish must have been too much of a wuss to call it quits. Because that's obviously what he wanted, right? I'm so busy replaying the whole scene in my mind that I almost slam the screen door on Wish, who has followed me. He catches the door with his foot and hands me my vocab book. "You left this in the truck," he says.

"Oh, uh, thanks," I say, wondering if that's wuss code for "we need to break up."

"Hey, man." Wish nods toward the bread rack, and that's when I notice Christian.

I do not want to introduce them, but Wish is standing there expectantly. "Wish, Christian, Christian, Wish," I mumble, waving my hand in the appropriate directions.

"Hey, man," Wish repeats, and stops rubbing his shoulder to extend his hand. They shake. Christian mutters some pleasantries that don't sound very pleasant the way he says them. There's a moment of silence while they just stand there, sizing each other up as if they're about to do battle, like all guys do when they meet. It's completely awkward.

"See you tonight," Wish says to me, breaking the silence. Then he jogs off to his truck.

The first thing I catch when I turn away from the display window is Christian's smug expression, big enough to fill the store. He starts to sing "Can You Feel the Love Tonight" from *The Lion King* in this horrible falsetto, using a hoagie roll as a microphone.

I glare at him.

"Well, at least you ditched the stay-at-home-mom look," he says.

"Shut up."

"It's an improvement."

"Could you please drop dead?"

"And leave you alone to take care of all this?"

I'm fishing for some witty retort, but nothing comes to mind.

"Scumbling screwfinger?" he offers.

I gnash my teeth so hard they hurt. "Whatever."

"Hey, where did you say he was from?" he asks.

I am not in the mood to discuss Wish with Christian. "What does it matter where a person is from," I say, putting on my best Christian bad-boy hiss, "when they're never going back?"

He shrugs. "No. Seriously."

"I am being serious." But he's still staring at me, so I give up. I need to get upstairs, anyway, and start prepping for tonight, which will likely take me every minute of the six hours I have left. "L.A."

He nods slowly. "Thought so."

I wait for him to say more. He doesn't. "Well, aren't you Mr. All-Knowing?"

He grins. "Tell me. Does he make you feel warm and kind of all hot and bothered whenever you see him? Do you feel a little delirious whenever he's around?"

I scowl at him. As if I would dignify that with a response. And anyway, it's not delirious so much as wanting to pee my pants.

"You do, don't you?" His grin widens. "Thought so."

Now I feel myself blushing. I need to run upstairs, stat, but for some reason I can't. I'm just dying to prove him wrong, to wipe that smug expression off his face. "And what else do you know about him?" I ask.

He scratches his chin. "He used to live here a few years ago, right? Well, I bet before he left, he wasn't all that, was he? He was just a regular old Joe, right?"

I don't say anything.

"And almost overnight, he's this gorgeous god, right? Everyone wants him. Am I right?"

I roll my eyes. "Wow, you have it all figured out, don't you? You should invest in a tent on the boardwalk and a deck of tarot cards."

He shakes his head. "Joke about it all you want. But the bottom line is, your boyfriend is trouble."

I'm reaching for a jelly donut and suddenly stop. "What do you mean?"

"It means that your boyfriend might have picked up a little more than a tan when he was out west. That he might be exerting a little influence upon you."

I squint at him. "Influence?"

"He's playing with powers he can't control," he says.

I squint even more. Does he know how goofy he sounds? "Um, like Lex Luthor?"

He waves a hand in my direction. "Fine, don't believe me. But these things never end well."

"Alrighty," I say, backing away carefully. Powers he can't control? We're talking about Philip Wishman, a guy who had an imaginary dog friend named Ruffy as a kid and could eat his weight in pinwheel cookies, not some diabolical evil genius. Wish couldn't harm a fly. And as this week has shown, he's so mild-mannered he couldn't even break the local fat girl's heart by calling it quits with her.

When I get upstairs, I'm not even in my bedroom before I'm tearing off my designer ensemble. My mom is in the kitchen, staring down the sink drain, but she whips her head up as I come barreling through the apartment like Tornado Gwendolyn. "Oh! You look wonderful. What a lovely out—" she begins, but I have the blouse half over my head and am struggling like a headless chicken to get it off, because I forgot to undo one of the buttons.

"I've got to take a shower," I mumble through the silky

fabric, bumping into the wall before pulling aside the curtain to my bedroom.

"Oh. Actually. You can't." By now I've freed myself from the blouse and am staring at her. She points to the sink. "No water pressure. I've called the repairman."

"What?" I shriek. Sure, things go wrong on a daily basis in an apartment that's as old as George Washington, but not the water! Water is one of those things I've come to take for granted, like death and bad caf food. So for this to happen today, the single most important day I've known thus far, is just . . . another chapter in the story of my screwy life.

She shrugs. "Since when do you need to take a shower on a Friday? Ohhhh," she says, raising her eyebrows a couple of times. "Hot date with Wish?"

"Mom. Ew." She still hasn't given up on her mission to help me get it on with Wish, but I'm too panicked to correct her. I start to do a mental inventory of everything I would use water for, besides showering off the crud I've accumulated from a particularly boring game of flag football in gym. Though I pretty much imitated a tree the entire time, it was hot outside, and well . . . as I mentioned, I'm a sweat machine. Great, I'll have to hope that my antiperspirant can perform miracles. Other than that . . . no teeth brushing. No flushing the toilets. Oh, hell, this is a disaster! And suddenly, I'm thirsty. "How long until the repair guy gets here?"

"He gave me a window of between noon and eight today."

"Window? That's like a giant black hole!" I moan. Okay,

time to reassess the situation. Water. Where can I get fresh water? Of course! Melinda's, next door. "Do you think Melinda would mind if I used one of her—"

"The whole block is out."

"Oh." I open the fridge and look for a container of water, anything I might use to work up a little lather with. Nothing. This is desperate. A car door slams. I run to the window and see a flash of red speeding away and Evie bounding up the stairs and smiling like she's in her own maxi-pad commercial, completely unaware of the horrors that await her once she enters the apartment. Beyond her, down the block, I see the dunes, and the boardwalk, where the beach entrance is. And right there . . .

A fountain!

A glimmer of hope ignites. Okay, it's been forever since I've been to the beach, and even when I was a kid making sand castles, that fountain was only powerful enough to dribble pathetically, like a drooling baby. Still, it's more than I have going for me here. If Mr. Repairman hasn't crawled out of his black hole to fix our water situation by eight o'clock, that's the master plan.

Meanwhile, Evie's face has just run the gamut from confusion to horror to denial, and now she is turning the knobs on the bathroom sink and moaning. As if she wouldn't look perfectly scrumptious after spending two months fighting for life in the Australian outback. I decide not to tell her about Operation Fountain and let her fend for herself.

At seven-forty-five, Mr. Repairman is still somewhere in a galaxy far, far away. I'm still in my cutoff sweat shorts and sticky bun–stained T-shirt, and Wish is going to pick me up in just over an hour. All I've done to prepare for the night is pop the pimple on my chin and eat another two jelly donuts. I feel drops of sweat dampening my forehead from the pressure. Still, I load up a plastic bag with my toothbrush, toothpaste, soap, and razor, and slip out the door. I don't think I'll have the nerve to shave my legs at the fountain, but who knows? I could get brave. Luckily, it has stopped raining, and the stars are popping out everywhere, bright in the sky. I hurry down the street, past Melinda's, and am just about to climb the ramp to the boardwalk when I see it.

Wish's truck.

It's parked right outside the entrance to the beach and it's covered in raindrops. What is he doing here? Shouldn't he be at home, getting ready for the party? Maybe he decided to catch a few waves with his board beforehand. That's the good thing about being a guy: you don't have to launch yourself off the cliff of madness, spending hours upon hours preparing for a party. Still, he is interfering with Operation Fountain. Like I'd be able to shave my legs there now?

My first instinct is to run in the other direction. Not only do I look like a goober in my ratty shorts and T-shirt, but I'm carrying my toiletries like a bag lady. But then I see his longboard peeking out of the back of his truck. So what is he doing out there? I can't help it: I find myself creeping toward the steps to the beach, toward the black horizon, where the gray storm clouds are moving out to sea. The wind whips through the dunes, whistling as it blows through the grass, and as the wet sand crunches under my bare feet, I see him. Not in his wet suit, on the waves, but on a dark blanket stretched out on the shore. He's lying there motionless, as if sunbathing, or worshipping, beneath the quiet black sky. The moon and the stars shine on his bare chest, making it glow yellow, like a lone dim bulb. I swallow, and the wind feels cool on the new sweat that's just sprung up on my hairline. Something about this scene is wrong. Not just that he's sunbathing where there is no sun, but that his chest doesn't seem to move . . . not at all. Not even to rise and fall with every breath.

It reminds me that I am forgetting to breathe. I take in the salty sea air and exhale slowly as a seagull screeches. Wish's body stirs and he springs upright, looking around. His back is to me, so I don't think he notices me, but he runs his hands through his hair, visibly shaking and tense, more agitated than I've ever seen him. He grabs handfuls of sand and throws it everywhere as a string of curses, horrible, vicious words I've never heard sweet Wish use before, spew from his mouth. He breathes once or twice, then settles back down again. Silent. Dead.

My only thought is That's not him. That's not Wish. I quickly make my way down the ramp, shivering all the while, wishing I could purge my memory of the last few moments. But I know that just wanting that means it will be etched there forever.

23

I MANAGED TO FIND ENOUGH SALIVA in my mouth to brush my teeth without water, and my legs don't feel too much like sandpaper. Well, at least they didn't, before I started to accumulate a goose bump per second, waiting for Wish to arrive. Now you could probably use my legs to grate cheese. And I feel like there's something hard and heavy pushing on my chest.

Speaking of not breathing . . . that had to be a mistake. Obviously he was breathing really, really slowly. Or maybe he was on the verge of dying. Yes, maybe he's lying on the beach, dead, and will not be coming to pick me up tonight.

There's a knock on the door. If that is him, he must have gotten over his childhood fear of our rickety staircase, because this is the first time in forever he's knocked on the door instead of shooting pebbles at my window. Beyond the lacy white curtains, I can see Wish's body framed in the porch light my mother leaves on whenever we're expecting company. Guess I can cross "dead" off my list.

I spend so long staring at the door that my mom gives me a look. "Hon, when someone outside knocks on the door, they usually want the person inside to open it."

I slowly walk to the door. The metal of the doorknob feels cold on my fingertips. I pull it open and try to look into his eyes but can manage only a quick glance at his perfect Adam's apple before I chicken out and fasten my gaze on his flip-flops. "Hi!" he says, so unlike that scary guy who was cursing on the beach earlier.

"Hey," I say. "Ready?"

I don't wait for him to say anything; I quickly pull the door closed behind us and keep looking at his flip-flops. I never noticed this before, but he has a pinky toe that likes to hide behind his second-smallest toe. "So what's up?" he asks me when we're sitting in his truck, as if he wasn't lying dead on a beach not an hour ago. His voice is a lot cheerier than it was earlier today.

"Um, not much," I say. Funny, though I still have an arsenal of topics of conversation at my disposal, the only one I can think of is Why the Hell Were You Lying on the Beach, Looking Dead?

His cell phone starts to ring. He rolls his eyes, reaches over with one hand, and turns it off without even checking the display. Then he shifts into first and clears his throat. "Oh, hey . . . sorry about this afternoon. I was just . . . in a mood. The rain. It bothers me."

I steal a glance at him. He's definitely back to the godlike Wish. The blinding smile is back, as is that glow in his eyes. No dead, yellow tinge to his tan, either. There's nothing even remotely lifeless about him. "No problem."

"Hey, I got something for you," he says, reaching across to my side of the truck. At first I think he's going to tweak my bare knee with his formerly dead hand, but instead he opens up the glove compartment and rifles around in it for a while. He pulls out a Madonna CD. Madonna. Like anyone listens to her anymore. "Your favorite, right?"

"Um, well . . . ," I begin.

"You mean, you don't listen to Madonna anymore?" he says in mock disappointment. Then he laughs. "You were her total slave when we were kids."

"I was a dork," I mutter, but have to laugh. "Thanks."

"Was?" He grins. "Seriously, though, I found this in my room. You must have left it at my house and it got mixed in with my stuff. Want it back?"

"No," I say immediately. As far as I care, he can use it as a Frisbee.

"Cool. 'Cause, you know, I listen to it. And every time I do, I think of you."

At first I'm thinking, How sweet, but then I realize that the song that probably makes him think about me is "Like a Virgin," which even my butt-tweaking of late has done very little to conceal. "Oh."

He stuffs it back into the glove compartment. We drive for a few moments in silence, and then, suddenly, Wish erupts, like he's been holding this song in forever, dying to let it out. "Open your heart to me, bay-beeee!" he sings. "I hold the lock and you hold the key."

Oh my gosh, he really has been listening to it. I screw up my face in disgust.

He laughs. "What's that look all about? You don't like my singing?"

I can't shake the image of him lying on the sand. "I saw you, you know. On the beach."

He raises his eyebrows as he shifts into a higher gear and we sail over the bridge to the mainland. "Well. Sometimes it helps me to think."

Think. About what? About how he's going to unload his ball and chain? I take a breath. "Are you trying to think of a way to break up with me?"

He pauses for a moment, during which my entire life flashes in front of my eyes, and then he bursts out laughing. "What?"

Immediately, I feel stupid, though I can't tell if that's a "What? Don't be silly," or a "What? Damn, you've got me figured out." "I mean, it's okay if that's what you want. Really." I put on my bravest smile, the one I've worked for days perfecting in anticipation of the breakup. Over the past few days, I've almost come to be okay with losing Wish as my boyfriend.

"Really?" He turns to study me for a second before downshifting. Then he sniffs dramatically. "I thought I meant more to you than that."

He pretends to wipe his eyes with the back of his hand. Okay, so make a joke of my impending heart attack. Whatever. Clearly this is not the best time to discuss this. "No, I mean . . . That's not what I meant. Just forget it."

We drive into a neighborhood I've never been to before,

with imposing stucco mansions spaced far apart atop perfect golf course lawns. Wish acts as if it's any old place, as if he's used to it, but I suck in what's left of the oxygen in the truck's cabin and grasp the armrest. I've been so busy lately thinking about Wish that I forgot I'll be spending the next few hours in the company of people who up until this week didn't know I existed. When we pull up to Terra's stately farmhouse with red shutters, I am dizzy. Still, I make it out the door without doing a face-plant into the unnaturally green and cushy grass near the curb. There is no way I am leading the way up the long driveway, past the red Mercedes convertible that probably cost more than my mother has ever made in her life, so I let Wish go first. He saunters up, like he belongs here, like he's royalty, even though he's wearing a worn black T-shirt and baggy shorts that hang on his frame like they belong to someone else.

We get to the front porch, where there isn't even one spiderweb in a corner or stray footprint on the creamy-white-painted wood-planked floor, and all the bushes surrounding it are pruned into perfectly smooth, symmetrical orbs. I swallow a few times to make sure I'm still alive, and then I see the little jockey statue hanging out among the greenery, holding a lantern. When Wish reaches for the door, I notice that the knocker is a bronze horse head. Then I realize that every shutter has an outline of a horse carved in the center of it.

I smile a little for the first time tonight. So what if I'm the only one in the world who gets the joke?

Wish looks at me, then at the knocker, and grins. "I've always thought it must be the portrait of a long-lost Goldbar ancestor, too," he says, reading my mind. "But don't worry. There's not a trough or a feed bag to be found inside."

He knocks me speechless. I can feel myself blushing. Okay, so I might have convinced myself that I'd be okay without Wish as my boyfriend. But suddenly, one thing is clear to me: without him as my *best* friend, I don't want to live.

24

WHEN THE DOOR OPENS, it's Terra and Erica. Terra smiles big, shouts, "Hey, you!" and opens the screen door for us.

When we step inside, I try to hold back my awe, but it comes out in one big gasp. There are a chandelier above us that has enough bling to outfit an entire Oscar ceremony and two huge staircases on either side of us, leading up to a landing with imposing iron scrollwork. I think the Von Trapp kids might come running if I whistle. The floor is white marble with a little black inlaid stone here and there.

Terra and Erica must have gotten dressed together, or else each had a dark moment, because they're both barefoot and wearing what look like identical black sundresses. Did they plan that? Isn't dressing like clones of one another a major fashion faux pas? After all the detail they went into this morning, discussing what they were going to wear, they had to have known they were on the road to disaster . . . right? Maybe there is a code for these things that says you have to look like you're going to a funeral. I didn't even check to see if Melinda's magic bag had a little black dress in it. I look down at my peach outfit and suddenly feel way too sunny and bright.

Wish gives them a once-over. "You guys look like twins."

They glance at each other; then Terra shakes her head. "Boys are so silly," she says to Erica, then places her thumbs under the straps of her sundress. "This is Nicole Miller. Hers is Betsey Johnson."

I try to smile knowingly, like I'm not one of the silly people, though I have no idea what they're talking about.

He raises an eyebrow. "Do they go to Cellarton High? Do they know you've been raiding their closets?"

They look at each other again, roll their eyes, and giggle, and then Terra grabs my hand. "Come on. We're all in the game room."

When I think "game room," I think maybe a few shelves of Yahtzee and Monopoly. But she leads me downstairs, to a sprawling room with a giant pool table, a Ping-Pong table, a foosball table, and . . . a shuffleboard? A couple of guys are playing darts in the corner, by the bar. Wish joins them and Terra flops down on a couch with a group of girls from school. They don't acknowledge me, because their noses and the entire lower halves of their faces are stuck in giant plastic cups. One girl starts crunching on ice and inspecting it. I think she asks Terra, "What is this stuff?" but I can't tell for sure, because some crazy dance music is blaring from invisible speakers.

"So did you hear about Destiny?" Terra yells over the noise to the group. "She's really sick. In the hospital. Her temperature was like a hundred and five after school."

I note that she doesn't seem worried about her friend, just excited that she is the one to convey this interesting bit of gossip. Across the room, in a nice secluded, dark corner, I can make out Rick, forehead to forehead with Evie. It definitely looks like she's put the "we're only friends" thing behind her. As if I didn't call that one a mile away.

I'm about to go over and, I don't know, beat some sense into her, maybe, when Terra jumps up and grabs what looks like a Dixie cup filled with lemon gelatin. By the time I realize what it is, she's already thrusting it into my hand. "Come on. You're way behind," she tells me.

"Um, I . . ." What would be a good excuse for my not drinking at the first party of my high school career, other than that I'm a totally lame spineless jellyfish? Actually, that's probably the best reason out there to imbibe. Let's see . . . recently had surgery? Am allergic to Jell-O? Had an unfortunate childhood experience involving lemons?

One of the girls narrows her eyes at me and whispers something to the girl next to her, something probably dripping with the words "lame" and "loser," though who knows? This is the new Dough; those words were reserved for the old one.

Still, I pluck the little cup out of Terra's hand. "Thanks."

I think that maybe I can go to the bathroom and chuck it down the toilet, but then I realize that all the girls around the circle are staring at me, waiting. I smile and then tilt the cup to my lips. It's Jell-O, so it just sits there. I squeeze the cup and hope it will come out, but still, nothing. This is clearly something one only gets good at with practice. I stick my tongue out and touch it. It's gooey and bitter and just the smell of the alcohol is getting me light-headed. Get it over with, Dough. Hurry, they're watching you. So I squeeze it as hard as I can and the whole giant glob tumbles into my mouth. Wincing, I swallow. It slides down my throat with only a little bit of burning. By the time I look back at my audience, my eyes are teary, and Terra is handing me another one. No sooner do I down it than the room starts to get blurry. The rest of the group goes back to talking and I try to act natural; well, as natural as a person can be when her esophagus is about to burst into flames. "Um, bathroom?" I ask Terra.

She points the way. I've heard there is an unwritten rule of bathroom etiquette that states that if you spend more than five minutes in the bathroom, people will think you are having stomach problems, so I exhaust four minutes and thirty seconds in this bathroom the size of my entire apartment grasping the edge of the sink and staring at my face in the mirror as it seems to bulge and constrict like a beating heart. Then I spend the next twenty seconds admiring the cute soaps Terra has, which are shaped and scented like pineapples.

When I emerge, wishing I weren't so on edge, because I would have liked to slip one of the soaps into my purse, I see the group of girls tossing back another round of shots and talking. Erica is licking her lips and Terra has her fingers in her ears and is singing "Do-Re-Mi" again. Hell, are they talking about Wish again? I look up in time to see him throw a perfect bull's-eye at the dartboard. He turns to me and smiles, oblivious to the horde of rabid she-wolves on the other side of the room who want to devour him.

Terra looks relieved when she sees me. She gets up and hands me another shot, then groans. "Ugh. He's my cousin, after all." I wonder if I can get away without doing this shot, but then she lifts another shot to mine and makes as if she's clinking glasses. "Cheers."

"Um, cheers," I say, then let the shot slide down my throat. It's getting easier, though feeling my feet is getting slightly harder. I look down. Still there. A little blurry, but still there. "So, um. They talk about Wish a lot, huh?"

She nods. "He's a bigger topic of conversation than Edward Cullen."

"Really?" I ask, more surprised that these girls read than anything else. No, they probably watched the movies.

"Yeah." She sighs. "It wasn't always this way, though."

I turn to her. "What do you mean?"

"Before he left for California, he was this big goofball. And now look at him. If you told me five years ago that Wish would grow to be a sex symbol, I would have said you were out of your mind." She shrugs. "Maybe there's something in the water out there?"

I shrug back, but I know what she means. It's good to hear someone else acknowledging it.

"Do you get sick of girls clawing each other to get to your guy?" she asks.

"A little."

"You should get yourself a bodyguard. Do you know what kind of sick things girls will do for a guy?"

I hadn't thought of it before, but tingles shoot up my back. Okay, maybe that's because I've just consumed more alcohol in a ten-minute period than I ever had up until this party, and tingles are shooting everywhere, even to the tip of my nose. My extremities kind of feel like tingly mush. Wish is standing across the basement, and suddenly, it seems like he's miles away, bathed in a halo of perfect light. Untouchable.

I'm going to retch.

His eyes meet mine a second before I turn and run. Back to the bathroom. The last thought that runs through my thick mind that isn't pure gibberish is To hell with the five-minute rule. I'm never coming out.

25

"YOU DON'T DRINK VERY MUCH," someone says.

Wish.

He's holding back my hair as I gag into the toilet again. Something yellow and slimy coats the bowl. "You think?" I mumble.

I look up at him. Somehow, even though I know I look like hell, I manage to look him in the eye. I must still be drunk. He hoists his backside up onto the marble counter and grins. "You passed out before ten. I think that's a record."

"I'm so proud," I moan. The buzz must be wearing off, because I remember I wore lots of mascara and run my finger over the tops of my cheeks. I pull it away and it's black. Great. I must look like a rabid raccoon. If I want Wish to fall desperately in love with me, this is probably not the way to do it. I sink into the bath mat and wish it were thick and luxurious enough for me to get lost in.

He's still grinning, and I can kind of see the goofy Wish who was left behind all those years ago. "Hey, don't feel bad. Can't say I would have fared much better."

I swallow, and my tongue feels thick, like a sausage. "What, you mean . . ."

"I'm not much of a drinker. But the way you were downing them, I thought you were an old pro."

I wonder what about little globs of lemon-colored goo tumbling down my chin said "old pro" to him. "Oh. No, I was just . . . I mean, I don't . . ." He's sitting there, as perfect as ever, patiently waiting for me to get my sentence out, while here I am, collapsed on the floor of a bathroom with my head in a toilet and all my Maybelline nowhere near where it's supposed to be. My cute peach dress is all wrinkled and the front is damp and yellowy from my puke. Even my perfect feet look veined and purple and weird in this light. So I can't help it: I crumble. "Don't you see?" I moan. "I don't ever go to parties. I'm a big fat loser!"

Now I can't look at him anymore, so I focus on his feet, which are dangling right at my eye level. Despite that one toe hiding, his feet are perfect, too. I hear him laugh. "I'd always heard alcohol was a depressant."

"I'm serious!" I snarl. "I don't get it. You've gone blind or something. You're . . . you're . . ." I wave a hand in front of him as I gasp for air between the sobs I'm trying to fight off. "You. And I'm me."

He raises an eyebrow.

"You're . . . perfect. And I'm not." I point out the door.

"And any one of those girls out there would kill to be with you, in case you hadn't noticed. Erica Dunleavy wants you so bad she drools every time she looks at you."

His smile slowly melts away, and a rare look of concern dawns on his face.

I stop breathing like a woman in labor. Maybe he really is so thick that he hasn't noticed, but even if this was a new revelation, it's no reason to be concerned. Most guys, on learning that someone like Erica was interested in them, would probably drop to their knees and thank the heavens. "What?"

He shakes his head. "Nobody's perfect," he says, his voice strangely serious.

"Whatever. Still . . ."

"Look, don't try to be like those girls," he says. "They're not you."

"I don't know what you're talking about. I'm not trying to be like any—"

"You know what I mean," he says. And yeah, I do. He's totally got my number. I'm a poser. But I have no idea how he can be so sensitive to my desperately trying to fit in when he doesn't even notice the extra pounds of my flesh that are plain as day. He stands and puts his hand on the gilded doorknob. "What do you say I take you home now?"

I sigh. Changing the subject. Maybe he is doing so because he realizes that the sooner he can get rid of me, the sooner he can move on to someone who doesn't have globs of yellow puke all over her. He opens the door a crack and I cringe. I can't wait for the "Who would have thought she'd be a lightweight?" comments. I was hoping that I could climb through the bathroom window to freedom; however, we are in Terra's basement and I am trapped like a rat.

He must sense my concern. "The coast is clear," he says. "The party's been over for hours."

"What?"

"It's almost morning. You blacked out."

"Really?" That sounds like something Dough Reilly would do at her very first social event of high school. When he opens the door, the room is dark. I can make out a few discarded paper Jell-O shot containers on the coffee table and it smells a little like cigarette smoke, but all signs of human life have disappeared. Guess I decimated the five-minute rule.

We get into his truck and pull away from the house. There's silence, and I can see him biting his lip in the reddish light of the rising sun. "What if I told you that—" His phone must be vibrating in his pocket, because he does a little dance in his seat and fishes it out, then looks at the display. He hands it to me. "The guards."

I open the phone. "Mom?"

She yawns. "Did you forget you were supposed to be here to help Hans this morning?"

And I didn't think it was possible for my stomach to feel any worse. I bet Evie went home and told her that I was drinking and puking. Like I need my mom yelling at me for the rest of the weekend. "I forgot."

"That's okay," she says, her voice brightening. "Did you have fun?"

There she goes again, the only parent in the free world

156

who wants her kid to be out at all hours of the night, engaging in unspeakable acts of debauchery. Still, I feel the need to explain myself. "Um, yeah. We all just crashed here for the night, and—"

"Cool. Just remember you need to help me clean out the freezer on Sunday. You and Evie. Let her know."

"Ev—?" I begin, but I catch myself. Evie isn't home yet, either. "Sure."

When I hang up, something immediately becomes clear to me. We're heading over the bridge, about a minute from my house. I say, "Wait. We can't go home. Did you see Evie?"

He raises his eyebrows. "She's not at home?"

I shake my head. "Did she leave with Rick?"

He shrugs. "I was in the bathroom with you for the last few hours."

He was? "Oh. Well. We've got to find her."

He motions at the windshield. "Found."

The bakery comes into view, and right away I see the showstopping red car. Hooray, I wasn't too thrilled at the prospect of going all the way back to the mainland to hang out on the perfectly manicured Rothman lawn, negotiating Evie's release. No sooner has Evie slammed the door than the car speeds away. When we pull up, Evie is still staring after it, a deer-in-the-headlights expression on her face. Then she wraps her arms around her, turns, and totters behind the bakery, oblivious to us. "She's so not a morning person," I observe.

He isn't paying attention. He throws the truck into neutral, jerks on the parking brake, and gives me a look like he has something important to say. But then he comes out with "You remember when we used to play hide-and-seek in the back of the bakery?"

I nod. "Uh-huh." I wonder if this trip down memory lane is going somewhere.

"Remember when I locked myself in the back room and ate all those pastry shells and then, by the time you found me, I'd thrown up all over the flour sacks?"

I laugh. "Oh, yeah. That was the last time Mom ever let us play there. So?"

He just shrugs. "I'm the same guy."

"Yeah."

"No, I am," he insists. "You put a piece of Spam in a Tootsie Roll package, it's still Spam."

I give him a look. "Yeah, but the difference is people will be way disappointed when they unwrap it."

He looks out the windshield, up at the moon, which is softly fading into the lightening sky, and sighs. "Exactly."

26

IN THE APARTMENT, Evie is sitting with her butt perched precariously on the edge of the living room sofa, staring at a six a.m. Saturday infomercial for some weird hair contraption that makes everyone who uses it, regardless of the previous state of her hair, look like the Bride of Frankenstein. She doesn't turn when the screen door slams behind me. "Hey," I say. "We have to clean out the freezer this weekend. Don't forget."

She doesn't answer, just sighs dramatically.

Ooooh. Trouble in Rick Rothmanland. I'm sure he finally realized that Rick Rothmanland wasn't big enough for the three of them: Rick, Evie, and Rick's ego. Score.

"Did he dump you?"

When she turns, there's a scowl on her face. "How could he have? We were never together in the first place." She raises her shoulder. "Besides, I always knew he was a jerk. I told you that."

"Oo-kay."

"And I was the one who told him I wanted to go home." She pouts. "So it's true. You were the one in the bathroom all night?"

I am sure that whatever the whisperings were—about me in the bathroom, ripping to shreds the five-minute rule—I don't want to know. "Um . . ."

"Wish was in there, too. Everyone was looking for him."

I don't bother to issue the correction: that all the girls were looking for him. "So?"

She raises her eyebrows. I'm about to ask her if Rick Rothman would spend a second of his precious time lifting her hair so she could puke, much less hours, when I catch her look. "So it was true? You guys were . . . doing it?"

"What?" I feel my face twisting. "No, I was . . ."

"You couldn't have been puking. Terra said you only had one shot."

"Three. I had three," I bluster, holding out the front of my dress to show her the evidence. I guess maybe leading everyone to believe I have this big sexual history with Wish now has them all thinking I go after it everywhere I can get a free moment, like a wild baboon.

"They were, like, mostly Jell-O, though. You could barely taste the alcohol." She wrinkles her nose.

I sigh and walk into my bedroom. It's probably better to let everyone think I'm a tart. I see an envelope on my bed. It's small, and "Gwendolyn Reilly" is chicken-scratched on the front in pencil. I pick it up and turn it over; it's sealed. Still inspecting it, I walk to the living room. "Ev, who did this come from?"

She's still watching the infomercial, but now she's sprawled out on the couch, eyes drooping. "Dunno. It was on the floor of the kitchen this morning."

I rip it open and see newsprint. I pull out a newspaper article, dread washing over me. Someone probably thought it would be funny to send me one of those "Gwen—thought you could use this!" notes, attached to an advertorial about some magic pill that will melt body fat. Reluctantly, I unfold it to read not I LOST SIX DRESS SIZES IN SIX DAYS! but SEA LEVEL UNEXPECTEDLY RISES.

I scan the page to the bottom, where something is scrawled in the same chicken scratch as on the envelope. I'm still expecting the fat joke, something like "Why, did you go for a swim?" Instead, it just says, "Thought you would find this interesting. —C"

Interesting? First of all, I think it's totally presumptuous and pompous when someone signs a note with a single initial instead of his whole name. I mean, I could have a hundred acquaintances with *C* as the first initial of their names. As it happens, though, I don't. I know only one "C." Christian. And he is just the type to do something weird like this.

But why an article on the sea level? What does that have to do with anything? The only things we've ever discussed in any detail are his mother's profession and my pathetic relationship with Wish. Like the sea level of Cellar Bay has anything to do with those. I read the first paragraph, hoping for some clue to the importance of this in my life.

CELLAR BAY—Experts say the sea level rose markedly yesterday, an average of 1.8 mm. The largest increase, of just over 3 mm, was reported near the New Jersey coastline. The island of Cellar Bay lost several yards of shoreline. This is of interest because though the sea level has been steadily rising, the previous increase has been at a rate of 1.8 mm per year. George Nichols, spokesperson for the National Oceanic and Atmospheric Administration, said, "The sea level rose only eight inches in all of the previous century, so obviously this is a troubling situation, and we will be watching this very carefully."

Global warming. It's a bitch. I scan the rest of the article with waning interest, wondering why Christian felt the need to bring this cheery news to me. What did I ever do to him?

The phone rings. It's my mom, wanting me to help bring the trays to the front. I yawn a "Be right there."

"You can take a nap as soon as the trays are set up," she coos, obviously proud that I had a normal Friday night for once, instead of staying in with her and reorganizing our sock drawers. "I called Christian and he's going to fill in for you. He's such a sweetie."

Oh, yeah, he's a regular jelly donut.

My head is throbbing. I guess this is what a hangover is. I change out of my puke-stained dress and nearly topple over trying to throw on my sweat shorts, then head down the stairs and into the back of the bakery. I grab a tray of Linzer tortes, and as I'm making my way to the store, I see Christian tying on his apron and shaking the dreads out of his eyes. "Thanks for the gift," I mutter as I pass him.

"I'm glad you think of it that way," he shouts after me. "Because that's what it is."

I place the tray in the rack at the front of the store and return. "How does the water level rising have anything to do with—"

"Heard about that, huh?" a gravelly voice cuts in. Hans, the baker, is standing in front of the machine that shoots fillings into pastries, holding two powdered donuts in his hands. "We might leave."

I stare at Hans. Hans is shaped like an industrial-sized refrigerator. His hands are like cinder blocks. He should not be afraid of a little thing like the ocean.

Christian nods. "They may end up evacuating us anyway."

I squint at them. Living on an island means occasionally having to boat out your front door, when a nor'easter makes the ocean swell and turns the streets into rivers. It just goes with the territory. We even have a permanent waterline on the brick facade outside the bakery, about two feet from the ground, from the last storm. Every year, when a bad storm is predicted, we're told to evacuate to the high school on the mainland, but we never do. Like my mom says, "If I wanted to hang out in a high school gym for hours on end, I would have become a phys ed teacher." Plus we've always been perfectly safe. "Overreact much?" I snort.

Hans and Christian just stare at me, faces grim. All I can think of is how awesome it would be if my name were Andersen.

"You don't find it troubling?" Hans says with his heavy German accent.

"Please. People here like to scream 'evacuate' whenever it so much as drizzles. You are all a bunch of wusses."

Hans turns to Christian and grumbles, "Did you see the ocean this morning? Never seen waves so big."

Christian smirks. "All of this might be underwater in a few days."

I wave them away. Hans has only been working with us for a couple of years, and Christian's just some goober from "out west." Nonlocals can be so paranoid. "It's happened before." I point to the black line on the wall. "This is where the water came up to inside. It was higher outside."

Christian nods, then reaches up and points to a spot over both our heads. "Let's see how brave you are when it gets this high."

"That'll never happen," I say, pointing to the black line. "This bakery has been here for a century, and that's the worst we ever got."

"Okay. But I hope you can swim, because you won't have me to rescue you."

I glare at him.

He bursts out laughing. "What? You've lived on an island your whole life and you never learned how to swim?"

I feel a growl growing in my throat. My father used to take me to the beach when I was a baby, but he left when I was two. Since then, I've been under the care of a single mom with a business and two kids. She never thought it worth the money to buy a badge to get onto the beach. Most of the time, I played around inside while she worked. The back of the bakery is a heaven for little kids, a gigantic maze of machines and racks and tables. Sometimes, after he spent a few hours on the beach with his parents, Wish would sneak over to the bakery to play hide-and-seek, or board games. Because it was better than the beach; you didn't have to worry about getting sand in your crotch or a sunburn. I'd planned to learn how to swim, but then certain things ended up getting in the way. My big butt, for one. "I . . . can," I fib, but I see by his face that he doesn't believe me.

Hans turns back to his donuts, and Christian continues to smile smugly at me.

"So, why would you clip that article for me?" I grumble as I pick up another tray, this one of freshly baked crumb cake. Somehow, even though I lost most of the contents of my stomach overnight, I haven't lost my appetite. I could eat half the tray in a blink. I turn to him and bat my eyelashes. "I'm flattered. I didn't know you cared."

He ignores me. "I can explain. This afternoon. Do you have time?"

"No," I say pointedly. Because if it's more crap about how the island of Cellar Bay is doomed to disappear under the sea, I would rather show up at school wearing nothing but a thong. But he's looking at me, for the first time, very seriously, and it's enough to make me curious. So I say, coolly, "Don't you think I have better things to do than spend time with you?"

He exhales. "Fine. I just clipped the article because I thought you could do something about it."

"Me?" I ask, wondering what could possibly have led him to so drastically overestimate my abilities. Shoving ten donuts down my throat in a minute is not quite a superpower. "What about me made you think that I have any influence over the tides?"

He hefts a particularly heavy tray of cinnamon bread loaves onto his shoulder and shrugs. "Maybe you don't, but you do have some influence over your boyfriend, don't you?"

27

THE STORMS START LATE that morning. The rain pounds the roof of our apartment, sliding down the windows in rivulets. We keep them open just a crack, because we don't have air-conditioning, so my skin feels clammy. It's midday, but even though my bedroom is dark, like just before nightfall, I can't sleep. I spend most of the time staring at the boot on the ceiling, wondering what Christian can possibly mean. He can't be suggesting that Wish has something to do with the tides. I never mistook the dreadlocked, Spenser-loving guy for sane, but this would make him completely off his rocker.

By one, when his shift ends, I'm dying of curiosity. I go downstairs in the pouring rain, drenching myself, and try to stroll into the store nonchalantly, as if looking for something for lunch. Christian appears in the door to the back room with a tray of sourdough loaves. He laughs. "Tip you over, pour you out?"

It's only then I notice I have one hand on my hip and one hand frozen in the air, kind of like a teapot. I drop my arms to my sides and say, "Whatever."

He starts slowly unloading the loaves of bread into the display case.

"It's after one. Your shift is over."

He keeps unloading the loaves, as if he didn't hear me. Jerk.

"Hello?" I ask, getting more impatient. "Can we get a move on?"

He picks up the empty tray. "A little impatient, are we?"

"I can't sit around waiting for you all day. I have things to do," I say. Like lie in bed.

"Well, aren't we popular?" he says in a sarcastic way that tells me he knows I'm not. He unties his apron, piles it on the counter, and heads for the door. "Let's go."

"Where are we going? Outside?" I ask, doubtful. After all, it's raining buckets, cold rain. I was hoping all the answers could be found inside the bakery.

He nods. "To the beach."

I sigh. Awesome. I never go to the beach when it's sunny and perfect, and he wants me to trek up there in a torrential downpour. I pull the hood of my sweatshirt over my ears and motion for him to lead the way. But I get three steps and I'm already soaked and shivering. The wind whips my hood from my head. This sucks. Anything he has to tell me cannot be worth this. "Hold on. Are you showing me something related to Wish 'playing with powers he can't control'?" I ask as we hurry up the block, past Melinda's hotel. The parking lot is empty and the Vacancy sign is blinking. Usually, she has guests staying until the end of September, but the place looks abandoned.

"Yeah."

"Okay." I turn on my heel and march back toward the bakery. As I do, I have to blink away the raindrops that fall into my eyes. "I'm going home. You're nuts."

He grabs me by the arm. "Hear me out. You'll want to see this."

I stop. By now, my hair is hanging in strings over my eyes and the hood of my sweatshirt is so heavy with water it feels like a cinder block around my neck. I think I could even wring out my undies. "I'm listening. Just make it quick. I'm getting pneumonia."

"There was an ancient race of people who thought that people's behaviors were controlled by the stars. Did you know that?"

I snort. "Oh, sure. I saw that on *Oprah* last week."

He ignores my sarcasm. "You can see evidence of it in the way people still think that full moons cause deviant behavior." He catches my confused look and says, "And astrology . . . it's totally based on the belief that the stars control human behavior. At one point in time, astrology and astronomy were one and the same."

"All right. But eventually people learned that astrology is a bunch of crap."

He shoves his hands deeper into his pockets. "It's not a myth. The stars do control our behavior. Our thoughts. Some of them, anyway."

"Really," I say, doubtful, wishing he'd get to the point. If Wish is being controlled by the stars, I'm Princess Leia. But then again, that would explain why he still hasn't broken up with me. I probably don't look as big from outer space.

"There was a cult in Europe in the seventeenth century that learned to control the stars, thereby controlling others," he explains. "They're called the Luminati."

"Wasn't one of the Indiana Jones movies about this?"

"*The Da Vinci Code*. And that was the Illuminati. Totally different."

"Oh." Still, I have never once been given the impression that Wish is inclined to bite the heads off chickens or drink blood or whatever ancient cults did. "Interesting," I say, "but not entirely applicable to our situation."

"You don't think so?"

"No. You don't know what I know about Wish. We've known each other forever. Wish is Wish. He's not part of some power-hungry ancient cult. Believe me."

"Well, the cult is still around. And it's all over the world now. He may not be part of the organized cult, but he may have learned their practices. And that's even more dangerous, the people who practice it alone, because they don't know all the rituals well. And I'm not saying that he would *control* control people," he says, a little flustered. "I'm talking about making people see things that aren't real. About him."

Things that aren't real? Wish is the most real, down-to-earth person I know. He wouldn't . . . "How do you know all this?"

"My mother was in Hollywood for a while. You said

that's where Wish lived. Some actors started using it in order to make themselves irresistible to their audience, and then their kids began using it, kids at the school I used to go to. . . ."

"Using it? What do they do?"

"It's complicated. But somehow they get the stars to favor them. Tilting mirrors at the right angle toward them . . . wearing certain clothes . . . spending time under the sun . . . It requires a lot of precision. Part of the art of it is learning to use the stars without throwing off the balance of nature. This"—he waves his hands in the air—"is because your boyfriend isn't particularly good at it, unfortunately."

"I'm sorry. That is really crazy," I say, but all the while I'm thinking about the past few days with Wish. How he wore nothing but black, which absorbs the rays of the sun. How he tilted the rearview mirror so the light shone into his face. How he was so upset when it rained . . .

"Think about it. There are millions of people in the world who read their horoscope these days because they believe the stars have some effect on them."

"Astrology is a bunch of crap," I repeat, but then I remember Wish's grandma Bertha and all her spells and crazy beliefs. Maybe she was part of the Luminati. She was really into astrology, Wish said, and when he first went to live with her in L.A., it really creeped him out. But eventually, he stopped talking about how nuts she was. I thought he'd just learned to live with it . . . but maybe he started believing in it? After all, he was always interested in the stars, calling me out in the middle of the night to come view them through his telescope on the beach. Maybe he . . . ?

"There must be some factual basis to it," Christian says, but I'm not really listening. "Humans always try to control things about nature. Don't you think that after all these years, someone might have found a way to control the stars?"

We approach the ramp to the boardwalk and climb up to where the dune grass is whipping in the wind. When we get to the steps that head down to the beach, I gasp.

It's gone.

Well, not *gone* gone. It's obviously high tide. Normally, there'd be a long stretch of white sand before the sea. That was how it was last night, when I stumbled on Wish, lying on the sand. I think about him sprawled there, in a space that is now completely covered by water. Now the water is lapping at the dunes, right before us. The lifeguard stand, once in the center of the beach, is barely visible in the black water. The ocean is angry and choppy, with whitecaps everywhere, and the giant waves, bigger than I've ever seen, boom like thunder as they crash to the sand.

"It's been like this before," I say weakly, though I can't remember when.

"Has it?"

I nod. "It's high tide. It will recede."

He shakes his head. "It'll be high tide in three hours."

"Three?" I swallow. "But what does this have to do with controlling the stars?"

"The sun is partly responsible for weather on Earth," he says. "And the sun is—"

"A star," I finish. "And this cult, the Luminati . . ."

"They're secretive, but they exist. But it's believed that

people practicing alone caused a plague in London in the 1600s. And a drought and famine in India in the 1700s. And in 1887 there was a flood in China . . . ," he rattles on, making my head spin.

"You're joking."

"I wish I was," he whispers very seriously. He turns his wrist and holds it for me to see. The rain drenches his skin as he points to a dark blob on it that would look like a birthmark if it weren't greenish. "Can you see that?"

I squint at it. "Unfortunate incident with a tattoo needle?"

"No. It used to be a star. The mark of the Luminati. I had it altered."

I stare at him. "You mean . . ."

"Those kids at my school. I was one of them."

"You were? So wait, what did you do?" I ask, my voice steadily rising. I can no longer keep the disgust out of it.

He nods, looking away, sheepishly. "It's not like we bit the heads off chickens, if that's what you're thinking."

"Um. I wasn't," I lie.

"My friends got me into it. It seems pretty harmless when you start. We would go out on the beach, late at night, and perform the rituals. We'd lie on the sand and wear all black to absorb the rays and the power of the stars. It may sound crazy, but sometimes the power of the stars was so invigorating that it gave us life on its own—we didn't need any other form of nourishment. We didn't need to eat or sleep to have energy; we could breathe without taking a breath." He pauses and inspects my face, which I know has lost all color. I can't stop seeing Wish's lifeless body on the sand, beneath the stars. Can his beauty really be only a facade? "So this is familiar to you."

"Um . . . no. It's crazy to me. It's not possible that a person, one person, could cause all this," I answer. "If you want me to believe you, you have to show me."

"It's kind of hard now. The cloud cover," he says.

"Sure it is. Fine. I'm going home. To sleep."

"No, you see, it's bad. Like a drug. It's addictive. I had to move away from them, convince myself that I could be anyone I chose on my own, without the help of the stars. It wasn't easy."

I stare at him. It's like he's trying to convince me that aliens exist without producing the little green squishy bodies. For something as way out there as this, I need the physical evidence. I think he understands that, because he finally sighs and pushes the dreads out of his eyes.

"All right. Fine. I'll show you. As soon as the storm ends. Okay?" His voice is strained. "I just kind of promised myself I'd never do it again, so . . . I'll only show you a few things."

"Okay."

He shrugs and starts to walk away from the churning black waves, and I take a few breaths, tasting the salty spray of the sea on my tongue before following him.

A car horn beeps. A familiar red sports car kicks up a puddle near us, but I don't feel the splash, because I'm already soaked. I stare at the car, too overwhelmed even to wonder why Rick would be beeping at me. The back window rolls down and I see Terra, wearing a pink hooded rain slicker. "Hey, girl!" she shouts at me.

"Oh. Hi!" I say. I was hoping to have the whole weekend

away from them so that they might forget my antics of last night. But it's good to know that my pathetic behavior didn't completely turn them off.

"You were hilarious last night," Erica drawls, leaning over Terra's lap.

"Oh. Thanks," I say, though I know they were probably laughing at me instead of with me.

"Did you have fun in the bathroom?" Erica gives me a wink.

Unbelievable. Everyone thinks I was in the bathroom doing things with Wish instead of puking or having stomach problems, two unfortunate things that would normally have hung around the old Dough Reilly in an impenetrable haze. Wish the Sun God and Dough, Goddess of Lard, getting cozy in the bathroom. The stars must like me and be working in my favor, because I can't imagine a group of people being denser. I peer past the raindrops on the front windshield and see Rick drumming his fingers on the steering wheel, like he'd rather be anywhere else. He has an arm draped around someone . . . someone with hair darker and curlier than Evie's. When he catches me looking, he pulls his arm away from her back. I can't be sure, but it looks like . . . Becca?

Becca. Evie's best friend.

Interesting. And yet not entirely unexpected.

Terra motions to the shoreline. "We had to come see this for ourselves. Isn't it wild?"

It takes me a minute to realize she isn't talking about Christian's bizarre theory about Wish's plans for world domination. "Oh, yeah."

"I love these kinds of storms," she gushes, rubbing her hands together greedily. Easy for her to say. She's living on the mainland. She looks at Christian, taking in his dreads and the tattoos on his forearms, and raises her eyebrows, as if we were just exchanging bodily fluids. "Who's your friend?"

I fumble through the introductions. Erica smiles and whispers something in Terra's ear, but it's loud enough for anyone to hear. "Rowr, the bad boy." Please. I should let him go all Oliver Twist on them.

Terra babbles on. "One minute they're predicting sun for the whole week, and the next minute, we're in the middle of a huge nor'easter. The people who live here must be freaked. They can't be at all prepared. I mean, this storm system totally came out of nowhere."

Christian gives me a sly grin. "Oh, I have a good idea of where it came from," he mumbles.

28

THE RAIN CONTINUES TO POUND for the rest of the day, almost like it's slamming directly against my skull, because I wind up with a massive headache. After the bakery closes, Mom comes upstairs and turns on the Weather Channel. I lie in bed, staring at the ceiling, only half listening to the cheery weather girl talking about "giant swells" and "gale-force winds." The other part of my brain is trying to wrap itself around what Christian told me. It's so stupid. Wish just has good genes and got lucky. People do that; I've seen people come back after a few months of summer vacation completely transformed, and Wish had a few years. It's not possible to fool everyone into seeing him as gorgeous and charming when he's not. And to cause a few natural disasters in the process. Not. Possible.

Since I've known Wish forever, we should be able to talk

about anything. I'm just making up my mind to come right out and ask him when the phone rings. My mom pushes aside the curtain in my doorway a second later. "It's your boyfriend," she says softly.

All the resolve I built up quickly drains from my body. Yes, I vowed to confront him, but not now. I get up slowly, hoping my resolve will magically return by the time I cross the kitchen to the phone. No surprise that it doesn't. When Mom hands me the phone, I see a worry wrinkle above her nose. "Make it quick," she whispers, her face serious. "We need to keep the line open."

"Hello?" I answer, nowhere near the confident vixen I've been trying to portray in recent days.

"Hey." He sounds drained. "What's up?"

I peek through the slats of the vertical blinds on our window. The water is raging down Central Avenue, like rapids. The curbs are completely submerged. Other than that, everything is just lovely. But really, "Did you make this storm?" is like "You have six weeks to live." Not exactly a conversation one can have over the phone. Plus my mom is staring at me, ready to pluck the phone out of my hands the moment the word "bye" leaves my lips. "Not much," I lie.

There's a pause. "Do you . . . want to go crabbing with me tomorrow?"

I burst out laughing. What planet is he on? I'm about to say, "Are you crazy? The waves are like tsunamis and the island is about to be washed away," but if he created this storm, he must know that. And if he created it, maybe he knows when it's going to end. "Um, the storm?" I ask.

"It'll be over tonight," he says. "I heard it on the weather."

I turn toward the television. Above the headline SURPRISE STORM BATTERS THE JERSEY COAST, a blond woman in a smart pink suit is waving her hand over a map of projected rainfall totals. Did he really? "But the water will probably be too choppy."

Although, not if he has anything to do with it.

"Humor me," he says, sounding exasperated. "I haven't gone crabbing in forever. I miss it. I don't care if we don't catch anything."

"All right."

"Pick you up at eight a.m.?"

"Okay." I hang up the phone and see my mother studying the television and chewing on her pinky fingernail. "Wish says it will end tonight."

"They're predicting it will continue until Wednesday," she says. Then she shrugs and turns off the set. "Mr. Wishman probably knows more than they do. They're always wrong. Either way, we're not evacuating."

"Is that what they want us to do?"

"They probably will. They always do."

Evie wanders in from her bedroom and grabs a bottle of iced tea out of the fridge. "The rain's stopped," she says.

My mother and I run to the window, since we don't believe it. It was just pounding against the roof a second ago. But Evie's right. The pools of water in the street are still, and the sunset is breaking through the clouds on the horizon. It's over.

Completely, one thousand percent over. Not five minutes ago it looked like walking out the front door would mean drowning. But now the fading sun is coming through the blinds, painting rosy red slashes on the living room wall.

The phone rings again. My mother answers and then gives me a curious look as she hands me the receiver, likely confused about why I am fielding more calls in a five-minute period than I have all summer. "I'm ready," the voice says, muted and serious.

It only takes a second to process. "Christian?"

"Yes. It's time. For the mission."

Great. Now he thinks he's James Bond. He must have been staring out the window, waiting for the all clear. I wonder if he's calling from his shoe phone. "Um, okay. The beach?"

"Yeah. Meet you out on the street in twenty." At least he doesn't say something goofy, like "nineteen hundred hours" or "let's synchronize our watches."

The line goes dead, and I check to make sure I have nothing between my teeth and walk down the staircase, trying to be nonchalant. Christian is coming out of the hotel at the same time. I hear Melinda's voice behind him. "You should bring a jacket! It's chilly on the beach at night!" she screeches. He raises his eyes toward the heavens and exhales long and hard. Leave it to Melinda to single-handedly destroy his James Bond image the way she destroyed my hair.

He's barefoot, wearing a black T-shirt that shows his tattoos. He has his hands shoved deep into the pockets of his baggy black pants. He doesn't say anything, just motions for me to follow him. "Um. Was I supposed to wear black?" I ask, looking down at my pink sweatshirt.

"Not a big deal," he says. "We're not really going to do it, anyway. I'll just show you a few things."

We get to the boardwalk and by now the tide is going out and there's a small sliver of beach. I kick off my flip-flops near the entrance and step down into the cold, damp sand, shivering in the wind. The waves are still big and choppy but they're not nearly as scary as they were earlier in the day. He walks with me toward an overturned rowboat and stares up at the sky. Then his eyes lazily trail to the sand. The footprints have been smoothed away by the waves, so it looks like we're the first people ever to come here. He drags his foot along, making a perfect circle on the smooth sand, stopping every so often to survey the sky. "Now, what I would do is walk around the outside of the circle, three times."

"Uh, okay," I say, keeping my opinions to myself. "What for?"

"It shows the stars you're welcoming them."

I can't help it: I was trying to give him the benefit of the doubt, but "Why not just bake them a pie?" leaks out.

I expect him to fire back a zinger, but he doesn't. He gives me a tired look, then stares at the horizon, where a few lights from passing ships blink on and off. Then, reluctantly, he starts to walk it.

"I thought you said you weren't going to—"

"If this is what it takes to get you to see that this isn't a joke . . ."

"Hey, don't blame me if you burst into flames or whatever," I say. Still, I don't stop him. I'm too curious.

"It won't do anything," he whispers. I'm unable to tear my eyes away as he steps around the circle, putting his heel directly in front of his toe, like a high-wire performer. I shiver and my breath catches. And maybe it's the moonlight bouncing off the waves, playing tricks on my eyes, but do the angles of his face begin to soften?

When he's done walking the circle, he pulls his shirt over his head. It's freezing, but before I can ask him what the hell he's thinking, he says in a rather breathless way, "Now I just lie within the circle."

As he's getting into position, I gasp. He has tattoos all over his chest. They look like stars, suns, moons, planets. When he kneels in the sand, I can see them on his shoulders, too.

I want to tell him to stop, that this is all too creepy for me, but I can't find my voice. He lies down and soon he is quiet and it's like I am the only one there, the only live person on the whole beach. Because suddenly, he goes still and then even his chest stops moving and I know he's doing exactly what Wish did. Whatever that was. And I know he doesn't really want to . . . he's doing it for me. I feel a stab of guilt for that. He said it was addictive; maybe it's like dangling a vial of coke in front of someone in rehab. It's been a few days since I was afraid of him; mostly I've just wanted to wring his neck. But gradually, as he lies there, open and vulnerable, I realize that a whole new side of him has been emerging, one I kind of like. And I sort of enjoy our verbal sparring matches, as much as I hate to admit it. I like him. So I finally find the words. "Stop," I murmur.

He doesn't. He continues to lie there. A seagull screeches overhead, somewhere among the darkening clouds, as if in warning. And then the stars begin to dull, or maybe that's all in my mind, because Christian's skin begins to glow. And at once it's no longer Christian. It's the image of Christian, his body and all . . . but it's him without flaw. His tattoos disappear. He's beautiful.

I double over, wanting to retch, but everything inside me is dry.

"Stop!" I shout, shaking his arm.

Nothing. I scream it over and over again, but it's like he's gone.

Breathless, I sink to my knees and shove him hard, so that he's lying facedown in the sand. He finally stirs.

"What the—" he says, as if I woke him from a long night's sleep. He rolls over and sits up, looking stunned. "What happened?"

"Okay, okay. I believe you," I say, unable to control my chattering teeth.

He rubs his neck. "Ouch. Good. Because I'm not doing it again."

"It hurts?"

"When you stop, it's like a hangover." He notices me looking at his chest, unable to break my gaze. "I used to take it very seriously," he admits sheepishly. "It's stupid. I wish I could get rid of them. They were just for fun. This is the only one that matters." He points at the star on his wrist. "I wasn't sure what tattooing over it would do, when I did it. The ritual takes longer, and I can't get the full power of the stars, so the effect is not as drastic . . . but I'll always belong to them."

"Belong to them?"

"To the stars. This mark . . . it identifies you to the stars. It says you belong to them. If you don't have it, it doesn't work."

"So you mean, I couldn't do it if I wanted to?"

"Nope. Not without the mark." He throws his shirt over his head, pulls his knees to his chest, and exhales. "It's funny. You start out thinking it's so cool, to be able to control the stars. But eventually they end up controlling you."

"And there's no way you can get rid of it?"

"No. Well, tattooing over it . . . trying to remove it helped. It made it less powerful. But it will never really go away. And it itches like hell sometimes. It wants me to perform the rituals. When I don't, it gets angry."

Angry? Who the hell would voluntarily get a moody tattoo? Wish is too smart for that. I think. "Wish doesn't have that mark. That star thing. Don't you think I would have seen it?"

"It depends on how well you know him."

I'm about to tell him that as a matter of fact, I know Wish really well, better than I know myself, so screw off, when he says, "It doesn't have to be on his wrist."

"Oh," I say, feeling stupid. I know him well, but not in the way that would allow me to identify errant birthmarks on his butt or anything.

My face must be all twisted in horror and embarrassment, because Christian smiles slyly. "Is he hot all the time? Like on fire? Does he wear all black? Does he get all pissy when it rains?" I don't say anything, but my face obviously broadcasts better than CNN, because he says, "He's definitely Luminati."

I swallow. "Okay, fine, say he is. How does he stop, then?"

"Everyone who plays with the stars has had to learn that attempting to use their power can have disastrous results. First, your boyfriend needs to learn it, too. Until then, he's in trouble."

I exhale. That's so cryptic. I was hoping there was a precise, twelve-step program for staraholics that I could get Wish to follow, maybe even anonymously, by stuffing a pamphlet in his locker. "Great. But how did you stop?"

"The hardest way you can, I guess," Christian says. "Cold turkey. I had to."

"Why?"

He looks at me for a moment and then breaks into a slow smile and shakes his head. "You remind me so much of my old girlfriend, it's scary."

I'm surprised. After all, he hasn't said much about his past life "out west," other than the whole belonging-to-a-cult thing. I figured it didn't matter much to him, because like he said, he's never going back. "Ravishingly beautiful?" I mutter.

"Asked too many questions."

"Well," I say, getting defensive, "I think a bomb like this requires them, don't you?"

He smirks. "There's another one."

"Shut up," I snap. Did I say I was starting to like him? Because now all I want to do is grab a handful of dreads and shove his head under the sand.

"She was really smart," he says, looking up at the sky. His next words are barely a whisper. "Smarter than me, that's for sure."

I'm about to say, "So she dumped you?" but that's another question, and I'd hate to prove him right.

So then there's a long moment of silence, during which I become aware that just about every pore of my body is bulging into a goose bump, screaming out for warmth. And since I'm not snuggling against present company, I stand up and dust the sand off my shorts, and the conversation is over.

29

IN THE MORNING, it's blindingly sunny and hot. So hot, in fact, that the wild rapids that were cascading down Central Avenue yesterday are nothing more than a few wet spots in the depressions in the road. But its ending so quickly is not nearly as weird as Wish's knowing that it was going to happen.

He picks me up exactly at eight. In the sun, he's achingly gorgeous. As I follow him, I start feeling dizzy and disoriented again. He looks a little nervous as he jogs down to the curb, jingling the keys to his truck back and forth in his hands. In the bed of the truck, I can see the nets, the traps, the buckets. He is such the little Boy Scout. That makes me smile. That is just like the old Wish, always prepared.

On the way over, we barely say two words to each other,

except when he offers me half his orange juice, which I decline. In his truck, I squint, more at him than at the sun, trying to see it. Trying to see the real him. If there is a fake exterior on him, it's a seamless one, the perfect disguise. We ride across the island, to the bay. There's a little rickety pier there, and a small beach with a swing set and a slide. The place is empty, though. Nobody in his right mind would be crabbing or fishing after that wicked storm.

Which reminds me . . . though the storm has passed, the water should still be a little rough. But it's perfectly smooth, reflecting the sky like a mirror, glistening in the sun like diamonds. Lucky us. Or is this the kind of luck Wish made?

"I brought the seine," he says. "Or would you rather just do it off the pier?"

"Pier," I answer. I do have on my ratty bay-walking sneakers, and I'm wearing my only bathing suit, an old-lady thing with a girdle inside and a ruffle around the middle, with cutoff jeans and a big T-shirt over it. But I'd rather stay dry for the time being. I never liked the water much, mostly because of the way it makes my clothes cling obscenely to my curves, but now there's something about it I don't trust. In fact, I trust it so little I've just about sweated through my T-shirt. "Is it really hot today or what?"

He shrugs. "A little."

"You must be roasting in that shirt," I say casually, hoping maybe he'll say something to put my suspicions to rest.

"I'm good," he says, and that's the end of that. I guess "But it's so awesome for helping me control the stars!" was probably too much to hope for.

I haven't been crabbing in ages. We used to go almost

every day in the summer when he lived here, but since he left, I've probably gone only three or four times. It just wasn't the same without him. We walk to the end of the pier and it's kind of like déjà vu. Everything is the same as when I was twelve, except Wish is beautiful. Or is he still the same but I'm not? He throws down a paint bucket and I grab the drop lines. "What bait did you bring?"

"Chicken necks," he says, holding up a plastic bag.

We affix the bait to the sinkers and toss in three drop lines and a couple of traps. Then we sit on the pier with our feet dangling off. "So . ... ," says Wish, and that's when my suspicions are confirmed. This isn't a crabbing-for-fun outing. Wish has something to get off his chest. Maybe he wants to tell me about the Luminati. Or . . .

The breakup. Of course! Somehow I knew it would come when I wasn't expecting it. And I've been so wrapped up in Christian's theory that I'd forgotten.

Fortunately, one of the lines bobs a little, so I interrupt him. "I think this line has one," I say.

He grabs a net. I reach down and slowly, inch by inch, pull up the line. When the chicken neck floats into view, there are two huge blue crabs nibbling on it. Wish swoops the net under them and expertly snares them. "Ha!" he says, pulling the net toward him and emptying it into the paint bucket. Then he tosses the line back into the bay.

He points into the bucket. "That one is, like, seven inches."

We stare at them for a moment, and then I get up the courage. Better get it over with. "You want to break up with me," I say softly.

He looks up at me. "What?"

I look away, at another line. "Right?"

He laughs. "I told you before. No."

"You didn't tell me that. You cracked a joke."

He raises his eyebrows. "Why do you keep asking? Do you want to break up with me?"

"Uh, no. I just . . ." I just want things to be like they were before you left. This is all so confusing. I wish we didn't have to have this conversation. I wish we could just go back to when it was him and me, in the back of the bakery, playing Yahtzee and our version, the G-rated version, of Would You Rather. But that's not possible. "I feel like there's something you're not telling me."

He reaches down and quickly pulls up one of the traps. It's empty, so he lets it fall back. "Is there another guy?"

Great, way to change the subject. I shake my head. Obviously he missed the fact that no guy at school, up until he arrived, knew I was alive.

"Because Terra told me something last night . . ."

Oh, right. Me and Christian. "What did she tell you?"

"She said something about seeing you on the boardwalk with another guy. Is it true?"

"No! Well, technically. He's that guy who works at the bakery. You met him. We were just talking. He was telling me . . ." Okay, now's the time. You can do it, Dough. "Um. When you were in L.A., did you ever . . . I don't know. Did you ever start getting into that astrology stuff that your grandmother used to talk about?"

His gaze trails down to the water. I can't tell if he's checking the lines or if he's just avoiding meeting my eyes. "What do you mean? What does that have to do with anything?"

"Did you?" I ask, pressing him.

"No," he finally answers. "Astrology is a bunch of crap. You know that. And Grandma Bertha is a nut. All my clothes smell like some crazy Indian weed that's supposed to ward off demons, because she stuck it in my suitcase while I was leaving. Why are you asking me?"

I can't help smiling as I shake my head. "Oh. Forget it. It's nothing." I stare at a rainbow kite bobbing in the perfect, cloudless sky. "Um. Is there something you want to tell me?"

He shakes his head and says, "It was nothing," but I get the feeling that it was something, and that I ruined it. That if I hadn't brought up the whole breaking-up idea, he might have told me.

We spend the next few hours barely talking. We catch fifteen crabs, which I let him have, since my family doesn't eat them. On the way home, we pass the digital sign outside the 7-E that gives the time and the temperature. It's almost noon. And it's one hundred and ten degrees.

In September.

One hundred and ten? It's never been that hot in Jersey before, even in the middle of July. No wonder I'm sweating like crazy. But when I look at Wish, I realize something. After three hours in the hot sun, in a black T-shirt, he doesn't look beat or weary at all. There isn't even a sheen of sweat on his forehead. He's cool as can be.

30

"YOU DIDN'T ASK HIM, did you?" Christian says when I walk into the bakery smelling like salty bay water and sweat.

I would normally have avoided Christian like the bathing suit department at Macy's. But the apartment is probably a sauna. The only place where we have air-conditioning is in the bakery. It helps a little, but the heat is so bad it's not enough to make the place completely cool. The sugar rings in the donut case glisten with melted sugar and Christian's cheeks and forehead are splotched red. I spend a few minutes draped over the ice machine, slurping down a carton of Nestea, trying to ignore him.

"Hello?" He waves at me. Then he laughs; it's this annoying, loud honking noise. "Your silence tells me all I need to know. By the way, nice weather we're having, huh?"

"Maybe I'm just not interested in talking to you," I say, angry at myself for even beginning to like him last night.

"Then why are you here?"

"Not for you." I bite my lip. "Okay. So he's wearing black today and it's really hot. And he has the mirrors tilted to his face. But—"

"That sounds about right," he says.

"I couldn't," I say, grinding my teeth. "I tried to bring it up. But it . . . I just . . ."

"It's a conversation killer. I know," he says. "You're thinking that if he isn't Luminati, he'll think you're out of your mind. But he is Luminati. I'm sure of it."

The thing is I'm sure of it, too. I don't know why I can't tell Wish that I know. Maybe it's because best friends tell each other everything, and today I gave him the perfect opportunity to get it off his chest. If we are best friends, Wish should be telling me.

So maybe we're not.

I sigh and head into the back room. A heavenly blast of cold air hits my ankles. Evie's coming out of the freezer with a stack of puff pastry shells. She has a little hot pink bandanna on her head, which makes her look like a cross between Aunt Jemima and Barbie.

"Did you forget we're supposed to clean the freezer today?" She makes a face at me.

Actually, cleaning the freezer sounds like fun compared to sweltering upstairs in the apartment. "I'm here."

She sets the pastry shells out on the table and wipes her brow. "What time is it? I've got to jet at two."

"Oh, yeah?" I wonder if her jetting away has anything to do with a certain egotistical jerk who's recently been seen traipsing around the island with her best friend.

She shrugs. "Oh, I know he's a jerk. But whatever. He has a Jet Ski."

"Well, that makes it all worthwhile."

She pulls the bandanna off her head. "No offense, but it's not like your boyfriend is such the perfect angel," she mutters.

"What's that supposed to mean?" I ask. Because that's probably why I can't believe anything Christian says. If I had to nominate anyone for Boy Scout of the Year, it would be Wish.

"Nothing." Her eyes momentarily catch mine and there's this weird look in them; she seems tired, peaked. Knowing that she's not the type to engage in heavy labor, I'm surprised. Maybe she's already done most of the work and I won't have much to do after all. "I've got to go," she huffs, walking off, looking almost . . . envious?

Could she really be jealous of Wish and me? She's tiny, but her footsteps pound like a jackhammer on the staircase outside. The screen door upstairs slams forcefully. I pull open the heavy door to the freezer and flip the lights on. Seems like the only thing she did was move the pastry shells, because everything else is one big disorganized pile. I sigh and get to work, laughing a little to myself. Really. Jealous. Of me. Who'd ever see that one coming?

31

AFTER AN HOUR OF CLEANING, I head upstairs to take a shower. Since I'm positive I smell like a combination of sea-water, sweat, and spoiled ricotta cheese, I really need one. But I find the bathroom door closed and locked. Evie's probably in there, doing one of her marathon eyebrow waxing sessions so she won't be furry for Rick.

My mom walks out of her bedroom, shaking a thermometer. "Found it!" she shouts to Evie.

Evie doesn't answer.

My mom knocks on the door. "Hon?"

Evie moans a little.

I snort. "What, is she sick?"

She shrugs. "She looks terrible. And she just threw up her lunch."

The toilet flushes, and a few minutes later, Evie appears

in the doorway. She looks the dictionary definition of "terrible." I never thought I'd ever be able to say that about Evie, but her skin looks almost purple and blotchy and her eyes are glassy and bulging. The glands on her neck are swollen like golf balls. I instinctively swallow. "Mom . . . ," Evie says miserably as my mother leads her to the couch.

My mother props a pillow under her head and feeds the thermometer between her pale lips. "She said some of the kids at school were sick?"

I nod. "Well, no, just one. It's not like it's an epidemic or anything."

Mom's already in the kitchen, pulling down a big mug from the shelf. "Hon, let me get you some tea."

Evie takes out the thermometer and groans at me. "I need to call Becca."

"Becca?" I ask. Oh, right. Her two-timing best friend.

"Yeah, she wanted to borrow my black top," she says, her voice hoarse and weak. "The one with the ruffles. For tonight."

I shake my head, take the thermometer from her, and push it back under her tongue. "Don't even think about her."

Evie spits it out. "She's my friend. And I know you don't know this, but friends look out for each other. No . . ." She starts to cough. It's a horrible hacking noise that I didn't think little perfect Evie was capable of.

"Offense, I got it," I say, watching her drift off. "So you knew that she and Rick were . . . together yesterday?"

"What?" I've obviously caught her in the headlights.

"Oh, yeah," she finally whispers, in such a way I can't tell if she's telling the truth.

My mother punches a few buttons on the microwave. "Let her rest. And get away from her. The last thing I need is you catching it."

"Don't give me that look," Evie says, though her eyes are so glazed I don't know how she can see a foot in front of her.

"What look?" I really, really don't have a look. I thought my face was completely blank.

"That 'I told you so' look," she moans.

"I'm not," I insist, though I am kind of feeling that way, but inside.

Her drooping eyes turn hateful. "Oh. Right. You were in the bathroom when Erica and your boyfriend were together."

I don't say anything, just shove the thermometer back in, so forcefully that she starts to gag, and walk away so she can't have the satisfaction of seeing my confused expression. She's delirious. Or jealous. Or maybe both. After all, Wish was in the bathroom with me the whole time. That's what everyone said.

Or at least, that's what Wish said.

I walk into my bedroom, trying to recall that night. All I can remember is flashes of the inside of a toilet bowl. I remember Wish saying, "I was in the bathroom with you for the last few hours." And Erica, at the beach, saying, "Did you have fun in the bathroom?" Did she mean fun with Wish, or fun with my cheek pressed against the porcelain of the toilet? How vague can you get? There's an IM from

Wish on my computer, and in it, he sounds a lot cheerier. A lot more like the friend Wish than the boyfriend Wish I'd been crabbing with earlier: *THANKS for today!!! Having steamed crabs tonight for dinner!!!* ☺

I mean, come on, it is not possible to get more angelic than Wish. Then I remember what Evie said. "Wish was in there, too. You guys were . . . doing it?" Right. So obviously, this stuff Evie's sputtering in her delirium is pure nonsense. Still . . .

"Evie, where did you get the idea—" I stop when I'm standing over the couch. She's asleep, breathing heavily, nostrils flaring, face half buried in a pillow. My mom's still steeping her tea, so I reach over and pluck the thermometer out of her mouth, since it's about to fall out, anyway, and read it:

One hundred and five.

32

AFTER MY MOM LEAVES with Evie for the hospital, I go downstairs to the bakery. Christian is sitting there, reading *Doctor Faustus*, another literary epic I'd rather pull out my own fingernails than read. Of course nobody in this weather is thinking about eating baked items; they're all inside, in their air-conditioning, sucking down iced drinks. "My mom wanted me to tell you she'll pay you tomorrow," I say.

He doesn't look up from his book, as if *Doctor Faustus* is so riveting he can't tear himself away from it. "All right."

"And can you close up? I'll help."

He raises an eyebrow. "I saw her speeding away. What's up?"

"She's taking Evie to the hospital. She's got a—"

"Fever," he finishes, then smiles with satisfaction at my

surprised face. "There's been a lot of that mysterious illness going around, I bet."

"Not a lot," I say softly. "Just a couple of people. What? Don't tell me you think this has to do with Wish, too."

He nods smugly, getting on my nerves. Next he'll be blaming Wish for his acne. "The ancient Italians believed that the stars were responsible for our health. The word 'influenza' comes from the belief that the stars influenced a person, making them feel ill."

"But that's crap," I say, seething. "All right, I concede that maybe Wish is doing that Luminati stuff, worshipping the stars or whatever. But just because he is doesn't mean he made my sister sick. It's probably just heatstroke. It's really hot out."

"You're right, it could be heatstroke. From the heat that your boyfriend caused. Just like the storm. Everything is connected," he says.

"He . . . ," I start, my cheeks flaring. "But what about you? You did it last night, too. Maybe you caused this."

"No. I didn't do it for long enough. And I did it the right way."

"So you're the pro and Wish is a dabbler. Okay."

"Basically. Are you afraid of losing him?"

"No, I'm—" I stop. I don't know what I'm afraid of. Maybe it's that if he went through all this trouble to make himself look good to others, it must be because he thinks looks are that important. "Maybe."

"But don't you get it? That's a small price to pay, considering . . ."

Something catches in his face at that moment, as if a bad

memory flashes through his mind. His jaw tenses and he exhales slowly, and then he shakes his head as if to shake away whatever was bothering him. I wait for him to complete his sentence but he just stands there, blank, the conversation forgotten.

"Considering . . . ?" I prompt.

He blinks and looks around, as if he's surprised by his surroundings. As if he's been someplace else entirely. "Considering what you could lose," he says softly, eyes trailing back to his book.

I stare at him for a moment. "You lost something?"

He doesn't look up, doesn't answer. And I don't think it's wise to press the issue, so I start to walk away.

"My girlfriend," he mumbles, still not looking up.

"Your . . . what?" I ask, my mouth hanging open. The girlfriend who asked too many questions. The one who I reminded him of. The one who I thought dumped him. "Are you saying she . . . died?"

His eyes narrow. "Do you think I meant that I just misplaced her?" Then he sighs, and his voice is barely a whisper. "She had a fever, too."

33

AT NIGHT, I'M ALL ALONE. I lie in bed, on top of the sheets, with all the windows open. There's a little breeze from the ocean but it's not enough. Thunder rumbles in the distance, and over the bay, lightning slashes the sky. Another storm. Another chapter in the most erratic week of weather this island has ever seen, which just happens to coincide with Wish's return to Cellar Bay.

Every so often, my computer pings with an IM. I know they're from Wish. Nobody else ever messages me. The first ones go something like this:

> Crabs were gr8 2-nite!
> Hey.
> U there?
> Hello?

U there? Msg me when you get in.
Did I do something wrong?

After a while, I stop checking. I just don't feel like it. Soon the phone starts ringing. He's finally given up on the computer and is now trying to call me. Persistent little bugger. I lie in bed, staring at the shadows moving across the boot on the ceiling. The storms . . . the heat . . . now Evie . . . If what Christian said is true, if he lost his girlfriend because of the fever, then Evie is in serious trouble. If Wish is responsible for it . . . How selfish can a person be?

No, no, he's not some all-powerful being. He's just Wish. Wish the Boy Scout. He's just human.

And all humans make mistakes. I think about what Evie said. Sure, she was delirious, but it made sense. Erica was practically foaming at the mouth over Wish. Of course if I was out of the way and alcohol was involved, she'd try something. And Wish is a Boy Scout, but he has hormones, like any other guy.

He never would have gotten involved with the Luminati if he hadn't at some point become as looks-obsessed as everyone else in the world. And he still must be, if he's still practicing their rituals. Any way you slice it, he's not the guy I knew all those years ago. He's different. And maybe a whole lot worse.

Something hits the side of my window. At first I think that it's my imagination, that I'm so distraught over losing the old days I'm hallucinating that Wish is at my window, but then I hear it again. And when I scoot to the end of my bed and look out, there he is, standing in the old flower bed, between two azalea bushes. He winds up like a baseball pitcher, then launches another pebble at the side of the house and whispers, "How long has it been since I've done this?"

I can't help smiling. There are a thousand little dings in the white paint of the shutters outside my bedroom. The stretch of yard between my house and Melinda's is nothing but tiny white pebbles that glisten in the moonlight, so I imagine he'd have enough ammunition to last him the next hundred years. "I'm the only one home. You can come up."

"Nah. You come down."

I look down. I'm wearing a hot pink T-shirt that says "Cutie" across the front. Perfect, if I were three. My mom got it for me on clearance at Wal-Mart and was so proud of it; she's probably the only person in the world who still believes that word describes me. But it's dark, and I don't feel like changing.

When I get down there, he smacks his leg. "Your house still has the most vicious mosquitoes."

"Thanks for inviting me to be a part of their next meal," I say as something skirts across my neck, giving me the shivers. Or maybe that's because he's looking at me, and in the yellow glow of the streetlight, he's breathtaking. It's moments like this that lead me to believe that Christian is telling the truth. Is it possible for anyone to look this beautiful naturally?

"I was messaging you," he says as we sit side by side on the ledge outside the bakery's display window. "I didn't know if you were home."

"Then why'd you come over here?"

"You looked pretty weird when I dropped you off today. I thought you were mad at me."

"I don't know. Should I be? Is it true about you and Erica?"

I've caught him off guard. "What?"

"Evie told me that while I was passed out, you and Erica . . ."

"We . . . what?" He rakes his hands through his hair. "Oh, God. Really?" Then he mutters, "This is such a mess. I'm a walking train wreck. It follows me everywhere I go. I can't escape it."

"Um . . . what are we talking about?"

He rubs his eyes tiredly. His laugh is bitter. "Erica's always been a spotlight stealer. Remember those horrible dances at the country club my parents belonged to?"

I nod, remembering the one I went to. The one during which I was locked in the dark bathroom and he had to rescue me.

"She'd always try to create some sort of drama. And she doesn't care who she hurts in the process. Spiking the punch, locking you in the bathroom, she—"

"She did that?" I ask, incredulous.

"Of course. She and her friends. I knew right away that it was them. And you know that reputation she has? It's all made up. All the guys she's supposedly been with . . . none of them can actually admit to being with her. Sure, they'd like to, but it's all a bunch of crap."

"You mean, that rumor about her making out with that guy . . . with her shirt off . . ."

He nods. "I think she started that one herself. Also, she's

one of those people who talks just to hear the sound of their voice, whether or not she has anything important to say. And she usually doesn't."

"Really?"

"Yeah. I mean, come on, have you ever visited her Facebook page? She updates her status so much because she's so high on herself, she actually thinks people care what she had for lunch. I was so upset that day to think that she was rubbing off on you. Don't let her. Okay?"

I nod slowly. "So it was a lie, about you and her?"

"Hell yeah. Who do you think I am? I have standards." His voice is low. "Gwen, people are going to say things to you about me. About the way I act. But don't believe them. It's not true. You know me. You know me better than anyone. Right?"

"I guess."

"No, look at me," he says. I try to meet his eyes but I can't get any higher than his chin, since he's so serious. "You do."

I nod. "Okay."

He looks up at the dark apartment. "Speaking of your sister, where is she? And your mom?"

"Evie's sick. Really sick. She has a fever."

"A fever?"

I look at his face, ready to gauge his expression. "Do you know anything about that?"

And I see it, in the second he averts his eyes from mine: a momentary flash of guilt, or fear, or something. Something not right. "What do you mean?"

At that moment, I know. I know that everything Christian has said is true. I know because this is the boy I spent years and years with, sharing just about everything two kids could share, from germs to stories to desserts to fears. And he, without a doubt, is afraid. Afraid of something. I spend a full minute staring him down. "Tell me," I urge. "If she dies . . ."

He opens his mouth, but nothing comes out. Finally, he says, "Why would I?"

I guess I do know him. And I know that while he may be telling the truth about Erica, he's lying about this. "Please stop," I tell him. "Please. You can stop it. I can help you."

He lets out a nervous laugh. "Stop what?"

So this is the way he's going to play it. Selfish, conceited, superficial, not the Wish I knew. "I'm really tired," I say. "Can we talk tomorrow?"

"I thought maybe . . . I was going for a walk on the beach. Look at the stars. Want to come? Play a rousing game of Gone with the Wind?"

I shake my head. It was the stars, the stars and him, that got us into this mess. "Sorry."

He starts to say something, but then nods and heads for his truck. "All right. Sleep tight."

As I trudge upstairs, feeling like someone beat the crap out of me, the phone rings. I run to answer it and it's my mom, giving me the update on Evie. She says that she's stable and that she'll be leaving her there overnight and coming home to get me.

"Get me?" I ask.

"Yeah, hon. There's a big storm coming. I just saw it on the Weather Channel."

"Huh?" I say, flipping on the television. There, just like before, is a cheery blond weather girl chattering on about another surprise storm that just reversed direction and is heading our way. On the map, it looks like a huge swirling mass of white clouds is about to swallow all of South Jersey. "Oh."

"This one is bigger than the last one."

I stare at the screen, motionless. Wish, Wish, Wish . . . what are you doing? "You're not going to . . . You don't mean we're going to evacuate?"

"Evacuate? Never. I can't very well leave you alone on the island during the storm. And I don't want to leave Evie, either. So I'm going to come and get you, and bring you to the hospital. Okeydokey?"

I say goodbye to her and I hear a rapping on the door. Between the lace curtains, I see Christian's dreads. For once, I'm glad to see him. "Hey," he says when I open the door; then his eyes trail to my pink shirt. "Cutie."

I try to slam the door in his face but he holds it open. "There's a big storm headed this way."

I let go of the door and bury my face in my hands. "And Wish caused it!" I sob, crumpling like a used tissue. "He's in total denial about the whole thing!"

He stands there, stiff. "Um. I just . . . I knew you were alone. I wanted to see if you were okay."

"Does this look okay?" I ask, leaving him in the open door and flopping down on the sofa. Then I quickly realize I am acting like a drama queen in front of a guy I don't even know that well, and sit up. "No. I guess I am fine. How are you?"

He looks confused. "Do you need anything?"

I shake my head. "My mom's coming back to pick me up and take me to the hospital," I say. "She doesn't want to leave Evie all by herself in the hospital and she doesn't want me to be here alone during the storm. So I guess I'm okay."

He nods, then makes a move to leave.

"Your girlfriend . . . ," I say softly. "You said she had a fever? Like Evie? How did she get it?"

He comes inside and sits down on the sofa beside me. "Yeah. We dated for a year, even before I found out about the Luminati. She didn't like it. She didn't understand why I had to be a part of it. I tried to get her to do it with me, but she said that it was stupid. That if someone didn't love her as she was, it was their problem, not hers. But she spent a lot of time with me, and she was a really tiny girl . . . and somehow just being near me, she got a fever. I never saw her. She got sick, her parents took her to the hospital, but by the time I found out what was going on, she was dead."

"That's horrible," I say. "I'm sorry."

"I spent a long time beating myself up over it. Then I convinced my mom to send me back here, to live with Grams. I needed new scenery. I thought it would help me to forget the Luminati. Forget her." He shakes out his dreads and laughs. "Little did I know . . ."

"Sorry," I say, watching the big white blob of weather on the television slowly inching forward, preparing to swallow the coast. "But I'm glad you were here to warn me. Not that it's doing much good. I finally got up the nerve to ask him about it and he denied it. I don't know what else to do. What would you do?"

He doesn't even think. "Break up with him."

My eyes narrow.

"He's clearly an idiot."

"How can you say that? You were Luminati, too."

"I didn't mean just because he's Luminati."

So he probably means because he's dating me. Jerk. I smack him on the shoulder. He gives me an innocent "what did I say?" look, but by then I'm dragging him toward the door by the hood of his jacket. "Go home." Finally, he stops digging his heels into the floor, shrugs, and obeys.

When Christian leaves, I think about the old days with Wish. How easy things were with him. I think about how we used to tell each other everything, and sometimes we didn't even have to. We'd just know. But this is clearly not the old Wish, because I have no idea what he's thinking. Why he won't just trust me. And when I think about that, I begin to cry. A few tears become sobs. Soon I'm curled in a ball on my bed, weeping and shaking with every noisy breath. Nobody is around to hear me, so I let go, and the tears fall all over my pillow and sheets until they're soaked. After a bit, with the first raindrops lulling me off, I fall asleep.

Soon I'm dreaming of storms and being close to Wish but unable to reach out and touch him. Every step takes me farther from him. I stretch my fingers out and grab him and his skin is so hot he bursts into flame, and begins to scream in agony. It turns into this long, low, dull moan, like that of a person whose life is slowly being drained away. It goes on and on, buzzing in my ears until my head begins to throb. When my eyes flicker open, I don't know where I am, what time it is. It might be only a few minutes later, or a few hours. My neck aches from being pressed against the head-board of my bed at an odd angle, which tells me I must have been in that position for a long time. But how long?

I try to sit up and I realize that though the dream has ended, though Wish is gone, his moan is still humming in my ears. It's not him, after all. It's actually the firehouse siren on the other side of the island. It blares, rising and falling, and though it's usually so loud it makes me cringe, the rain is pounding loudly enough against the roof to nearly drown it out.

"Mom?" I call out.

No answer. Instead, something crashes inside the house. I jump to my feet in the darkness, jarred into action. What is going on?

I stumble across my room and flick the light switch a few times, but nothing happens. We must have lost power. The wind tears through the curtains, whistling fiercely. I fight it to close the window, and at the same time a bolt of lightning flashes and a boom of thunder crashes, throwing me back to the bed.

Lights flash outside, on the road. I crawl to the window and peek over the ledge. A line of three or four cars is slowly making its way through the rain, toward the bridge. The cars cut through the rushing water, and in the headlights, I see it's already spilling over the curbs.

Where is my mother? She was supposed to come home. She was supposed to come and wake me and take me to the hospital.

Then I realize something. The siren. How many times did it sound? It seemed like it went on forever. And forever means . . .

My mom told me that. It sounds once every day at noon. Three times for a fire. And seven times . . . Seven times is the call to evacuate.

Evacuation. The cars are heading toward the bridge because there is an evacuation effort under way. I wonder how long it has been going on. I couldn't have slept through the siren's sounding . . . could I have? I rush to the window again. The houses in the distance are barely visible. There are no more cars on the road, no lights cutting through the darkness. It's as if I'm the only one on the island.

I remind myself what my mom said. They always call to evacuate when it's not really necessary. They always play it safe. I'm sure it's not a problem.

Still . . .

I reach for the phone. Who do I call? My mom doesn't have a cell. Wish. I'll call Wish. So what if he's different? He's all I have.

I bring the receiver up to my ear. No dial tone.

Not good.

Stumbling around as the wind pummels the side of the building, I manage to close all the windows and find the flashlight in a kitchen drawer. I sit down on the couch for a minute, wondering what I should do. The only thing that comes to mind is curling into a ball again, but this time, sobbing for my mommy. I start imagining the worst: the water rising steadily until all the furniture in our second-floor apartment floats out to sea, a huge tsunami engulfing the island, giant sea turtles coming ashore to eat me.

No, be calm, Dough. This storm will pass and everything will be fine.

A light flickers outside. I run to the window; outside the hotel, someone is helping Melinda into the passenger side of her ancient Lincoln Town Car. Christian!

Moving quickly, I grab the flashlight, aim it in his direction, and turn it on and off a few times in Morse code fashion. Not that I know Morse code, but whatever. Then I run to the door. I'm nearly drenched before it slams shut behind me. I cup my hands around my mouth. "Christian!" I scream. Then I wave my hands.

He tilts his chin up toward me. I think he sees me.

"Wait for me!" I turn back to the apartment. I'm sure he'll wait. Okay, do I need to take anything with me? I'm still wearing my pink Cutie tee. I look down. My nipples are standing at attention. The fabric of the shirt is so sheer I can almost see the tiny goose bumps surrounding my nipples, peeking through the fabric.

I cannot leave the house looking like this.

"One second!" I shout down to him as he wades— wades?—to the driver's side of the car. The water is over his knees. How can that be? How long was I asleep? Is this a dream? "I have to get something!"

I rush inside, feeling my way, then stub my toe on the kitchen table. Cursing and hopping like a demented rabbit, I find my lingerie drawer and manage to untangle a bra from the panties and socks in there. Then I pull off my wet tee, strap in the girls, and throw on the only shirt I can find, shorts, a Windbreaker, and flip-flops. Anything else? Anything else? I can't think.

I trip over that same evil leg of the kitchen table on the way out. Cursing and hopping some more, I open up the screen door and run out into the driving rain. And before I can make it down two or three steps, I realize something.

Everything is dark. The Town Car isn't idling in the driveway as I expected, with its two headlights cutting through the weather. Lightning flashes, making the street bright as day, but it's empty. There is no sign of life outside, no cars approaching on the road, nothing. Nothing on the island but the rising storm, and me.

He left me.

34

OKAY, maybe he went down the street to get gas or something. Maybe he'll be right back.

Now I can't even be sure he did see me. I thought he did, but maybe he didn't. I was in such a rush to grab a bra and save myself from the embarrassment of nipple exposure I didn't make sure he knew I was here. And if he didn't see me, then . . .

I am screwed.

No, no. They're always evacuating this island. This is nothing! No big deal!

I keep repeating No big deal! as I make my way down the staircase at the side of the building, hoping that when I peek around the corner, the car will be waiting for me in front. Christian will laugh and say, "What took you so long?" and in two seconds I will have the hot air from the Town

Car's heater aimed right at my face, roasting my cheeks a sunny red. At the third step from the bottom, though, the staircase disappears into black water. Cringing, I step down until it laps at my ankles. It's not entirely cold, but it's not a nice, warm, toasty heater. The next step, it's up to my knees. I slide off the staircase into water that's up to my thighs, then wade out onto the sidewalk, or where the sidewalk used to be. The gusts of wind make waves in the water, and the force nearly pushes me back against the crumbling brick wall of the bakery, but slowly I manage to fight it. But the street is empty, and now it's just a river, not a place where cars could safely travel. In the distance, the one stoplight on the island is swaying in the wind, blinking red and taunting me. I stop chanting No big deal, and stifle a sob.

All right, I tell myself, trying to push down the ugly head of fear that keeps intervening. Concentrate. But all I can think of is the look Christian gave me when I called to him. It was blank; he was blinking away the raindrops that were falling in his face. Of course he didn't see me. If he had, he would have helped me. Or maybe he would have laughed at me. After all, what was it I had told him? Something like, "Stop overreacting. We never evacuate."

I am a total dumb ass.

The siren begins again. Oh, you want me to evacuate, Mr. Noisy Siren? That's what I'm trying to do. Big help you are. My face is soaked with rain, and I'm crying. And shivering. And doing all those things one isn't supposed to do in a crisis.

When the siren ebbs, I hear something. Ringing. The phone.

It must be working again. Or I'm hallucinating in my hysteria. I start to run up the stairs, but the sound fades. Then I realize it's not the phone in the apartment that's ringing. It's the one in the bakery.

I quickly reverse direction, tripping over my own feet and nearly launching myself right into the floodwater. I catch myself and wade slowly back in, pulling open the side door to the bakery. Compared to outside, it's graveyard quiet here, except for the ringing of the phone. The water in here is stagnant, black, and I splash through it up to my knees. It smells like cinnamon sugar laced with salt water. Some empty milk jugs and other debris are bobbing happily in it. I push past them and grab the receiver. "Hello?" I say, my voice squeaky and not at all calm.

But I'm speaking to a dial tone.

It's okay, I think, pounding on the hook a few times. I'll just call 911.

Fingers shaking, I find the buttons, then curse when I hear "All circuits are busy." How can that be? Isn't 911 supposed to work no matter what?

The phone rings again. I pick it up immediately. "Hello?"

"Gwen?"

"Wish?"

The siren starts up again. Inside, it sounds quieter, but it still rattles in my eardrums.

"Yeah. Are you okay? What's that noise?"

I can't help it: I start to bawl. "No!" I blubber, but I sound like a weepy Santa Claus: No-ho-ho-ho-ho. "It's the evacuation signal! Everything's flooding! My mom was supposed to come and pick me up but she never showed up and I must have slept through the evacuation! I'm here all alone and there's no power and I don't know what to do."

"Okay, calm down. Call 911."

"I tried. It won't let me through."

"Can you wave down a police officer or something?"

I sniff. "There's nobody here. Everyone's gone!"

He exhales. "There's a fire on the other side of the island. I bet all the emergency workers are there."

"Can you . . ." My voice is small. "Can you stop it?"

There's a pause. "Me?" His voice is smaller yet.

I know how stupid it sounds. Like Wish could just flip a switch, and all this will be gone. But he did it before. At least, he knew when the last storm was going to end. He knows things. Maybe he knows how to end this. "Then can you come get me?"

"Well, I saw on the news that they're not letting anyone on the island. . . ."

At that, I start to cry again. He can't save me. Of course he can't. He's only human, after all. "What am I going to do? I can't swim, and—"

"Gwen, listen to me," he says, his voice firm. "Go upstairs to the apartment. If the water comes in there, try to get onto the roof. Okay?"

"But what if—"

"Listen to me," he repeats, his voice calm. "Nothing is going to happen to you. I won't let it. I'm on my way."

"But you said they weren't letting anyone on the island."

"I'm on my way," he repeats. "Go up to your apartment. I'll see you soon."

And then he hangs up, before I can turn any of the thousands of thought fragments buzzing through my head into words. Out in the storm again, I wade to the staircase leading to the apartment. The rain is falling harder than ever, and water is now over the first five steps, up to my waist. I don't care how manly Wish's truck is—it can't cut through this. Is he planning on swimming here? Still, he's a man of his word, and right now, it's all I have.

35

AN HOUR LATER, I'm still cold and wet, sitting in the apartment, watching the gradually lightening sky out the window. I think it might be almost morning, but it's hard to tell, since the clouds are so dark. I've gotten pretty good at ignoring the sirens when I hear a new noise. It sounds like the ocean. In the winter, when the ocean is choppy and rough and the wind is blowing from the east, if a person stands outside, he can sometimes hear the waves crashing as if he's standing right atop the surf.

Then something crashes against the side of the building, shaking all the walls. A loud clap of thunder sounds and the floor begins to pitch. I throw myself down beside the couch. With my cheek pressed against the linoleum, I hear it again, almost as if I'm right on the sand: the ocean. Another crash, and another. The house shudders with every noise.

I swallow as I stand and move toward the back window, the one in the bathroom. It's small and frosted and we never open it, but I remember that it does have a little view of the ocean, if you look past the roof of the south wing of Melinda's hotel. Well, not the ocean, but the boardwalk, and beyond that, the softly rising dunes, spotted with grass. The humid weather makes everything stick in this house, especially the old windows, so I force it up with the heel of my hand, almost knowing what I'll find there. When I crane my neck, it's even worse. The dunes are gone. It's nothing but sea.

All that's there, among the waves, is the top of Melinda's hotel.

I gasp as a small wave passing the hotel separates, then comes toward the apartment. It splashes me as it crashes against the side of the apartment. Our bakery is in the middle of the ocean.

And not only that . . . in the distance I see something I've only seen in movies. I'm a Jersey girl, and these things don't happen in Jersey, but I'm almost positive that beyond the shoreline, I see a gray funnel weaving its way across the horizon.

A freaking tornado.

A sinking realization hits me. Wish isn't coming. How could he? Even if he wanted to, it would be impossible. He'd need a rescue helicopter or something. My only hope is that he got through to emergency services and they are on their way. But are they? Even with a helicopter or a rescue boat, nobody would steer themselves right into a tornado.

Wish's words ring in my ears. Do I go up to the roof? Is

it safer there? How do I get up there? I turn and see the water lapping at the bottom pane of the window, like I'm looking into a giant fishbowl.

I can't stay here.

I throw my Windbreaker back on, pull open the heavy wood door, and shriek. Water pours through the screen door, into the kitchen. I try to push it open, but the water is too much. It won't budge. I whirl around and run toward the window over my bed, and it rattles as it opens, scaring a few seagulls from their place of refuge. Some water pours in, but I can at least get through it. I crouch on my bed, trying to get up the courage to climb onto the ledge and hoist myself up to the roof as water pools on my sheets and comforter. The edge of the window digs into my feet as I position them there, then reach up toward the eave, looking for a gutter or something else to hold on to. The white peeling paint catches in my fingernails as I grab for the gutter, but it's not close enough to use to lift myself. I'd have to swim out and get ahold of it that way, but I'd sink like a rock.

But I need to go. I can't stay here. I taste blood on my lips and realize I've chewed them raw. I can maybe doggie-paddle my way out a few feet, and then I can quickly reach up and grab that gutter, as long as a wave doesn't carry me away. I look over my shoulder. The water is covering the linoleum.

I try to imagine Wish standing near me. It's the next-best thing to him, I think, because at this moment, I don't think I'll ever see him again. I swallow the sob in my throat.

A wave slides by under the window, and then the water subsides a bit. It seems calmer, maybe deceptively so. My fingernails digging into the sides of the window frame, I silently say a prayer. I let go.

I paddle. I reach. I see a wave, over my head. I taste salt. I see the white foam above me, and then everything is tinged in green, like in a dream.

36

"Gwen?" A soft voice pulls me back.

Wish.

He's standing over me, his eyebrows arched in concern. Everything around me is white, plastic. Beyond him is the sky, just as blue and cloudless as on a perfect summer morning. The world around me pitches and tosses, making my stomach feel queasy.

"Oh, thank God," he says. "How are you?"

The sun burns my forehead and nose. My throat feels like I've been sucking on razor blades. My skull feels like it's being squeezed in a vise. I sit up and rub my head, but my hair is gritty and matted and wet. Everything around me is clammy and uncomfortable. When I blink a few times, I realize we are on a boat, rocking in the middle of the sea. I try to remember where I was the moment I lost conscious-ness, but I can't. When did I decide to go on a boating trip with Wish? How did I get here?

"Wish? Where are we?"

That's when I see it, only a few yards away: the roof of a building. A familiar one. Melinda's hotel. It's the only thing visible on our island except the enormous flag that flies high over the firehouse, looming in the distance, a few feet above the waves. These are the only things not under-water.

Suddenly, it hits me. The storm. The tornado. Climbing out onto the windowsill and slipping into the black waves. And Wish. Wish, who caused it all.

I turn to him, shivering uncontrollably in my wet T-shirt. But he is no longer looking at me; he's staring at the horizon, toward where the shoreline usually is. But it's not there, either. I can hear the wind whipping in the dis-tance. Raging all around us. But not here. Not where we sit, on a fairly calm ocean, under a sun-filled sky.

We're in the eye of the storm.

"Wish," I say. But he keeps his eyes fastened on the sky. Commanding it. "Wish! What are you doing?"

He bites his lip. "I will not let anything happen to you." His voice is strained. "Don't worry."

I'm worrying. I'm more than worrying. I stand, rocking with the waves, and put my hand on his shoulder. He tries to shake it free, his eyes never leaving the wild squall upon us. "I know everything!" I shout at him. "I know all about the Luminati!"

He turns to me. "What?"

"I know," I say. "I know that you're using the stars to change the way people see you. Stop it. You have to stop it now."

"No," he shouts back. "I can't. You don't understand—"

"Of course I do. You think I don't understand what it's like to be ordinary?" I ask him, trying to keep my balance.

He doesn't answer. My head pounds. The boat pitches again. I lose my footing, toppling backward. The last thing I remember is two screeching seagulls circling above, stark white against the sky, a sky black and menacing, waiting to close in on us.

37

SOMETIME LATER—it feels like years—I open my eyes again. A ceiling greets me. I'm inside, but somewhere I don't recognize. Everything is white. A hospital. There's a television mounted to the wall, with some news program on; a white-haired reporter is droning on about politics.

"Hey, hon." It's my mom. She fluffs my pillows. "You have a bump on the head. How do you feel?"

I groan. My head throbs. I reach up to touch it and feel sand in my hairline. Everything at the bakery—the flooding, the boat with Wish—seems like a faraway memory. The bakery. "What happened to our house?"

She shrugs. "I hear it's not very pretty. But thank goodness you're safe."

I remember Wish's promise to come get me. Did he? Or was that a dream?

I scan the room, but I already know that my mom is the only person here. I think of the blinding sun making a halo around Wish's head as he commanded it, with the black storm clouds swirling around us. I remember the entire island, save for the top of Melinda's hotel, being underwater. That had to have been a dream. There is no way on Earth any of that could possibly have happened. "How did I get here?" I ask.

"The coast guard had you airlifted here by helicopter. I'm sorry I wasn't there. I tried," she whispers. "The island was closed; they wouldn't let anyone on. They said everyone had been evacuated. I tried calling you again, but when you didn't answer, I thought you must have gotten a ride to the high school with Melinda. But then I went to the gym to look for you, and you weren't there. . . . I was so worried." She buries her face in her hands.

"I think I must have slept through the evacuation," I say, feeling stupid. "I woke up and the water was already so high. And everyone was gone."

She nods. "By the time I found out you weren't there and told the police so they knew to look for you, the wind was too much. They couldn't go, either."

I shake my head. My vision is blurred, and maybe there's water in my ears, because nothing makes sense. "So they called the coast guard?"

She nods. "But they couldn't get out there right away. There was a tornado."

Oh, so the tornado was real? I was thinking that had to have been part of the dream, too. "I remember the water coming up into the apartment. And then I tried to climb out onto the roof. And then . . ." I swallow, and I can still taste salt. It's all hazy, but I clearly remember the flash of fear from losing my footing. Tumbling into the water, everything in my sight washing green-gray. Fighting to stay above the waves. "I fell in. But somehow I must have gotten onto the roof. I guess. I have no idea how."

"Well, you're safe now." She plants a kiss on my forehead, I think because my Nancy Drew meanderings are getting me a little worked up. "Just rest."

Still, the more I think about it, the more I know it's a miracle I was able to get out of the water. "But . . ."

"I think you were lucky the boat came along."

My ears prick up. "Boat? You mean Wish?"

And then he walks in, carrying a big bouquet of balloons. "Duh."

"Oh" is all I can get out at first. I feel like I haven't seen him in ages, because my heart starts to flutter. I don't think I've ever been so glad to see him. "Was that your dad's boat?"

"Yeah," he says with a smile. "It's more like a yacht, if you ask him. And I'm going to be grounded for the rest of my life. He never lets me use the thing."

He looks different somehow. For the first time, he's wearing something other than that black shirt—a white crumpled tee that he probably slept in and equally wrinkled khaki shorts. He deposits the bouquet on the radiator under the window and sits beside me. "What's up?" he asks, taking in my expression.

"Um. You got me out?" I ask.

He looks at me like I've grown antlers. "I said I would."

"But there was a . . . tornado."

He smirks. "I didn't say it was easy."

"Thank you," I whisper.

"Hey. That's what friends are for, right?" He says it like he just offered me half of his Tastykake.

My mom backs toward the door. "Well. Better go check on Evie," she says.

That's right. Evie. Suddenly, it comes to me: Evie's sick. "Is she . . ."

"She's fine. Her fever is down," my mom says before ducking out of the room.

Wish is sitting beside me, looking sheepish. He saved me . . . because he had to. He knows he's guilty. All those suspicions must be evident on my face, because he narrows his eyes and says, "I'm sorry, Gwen. I would have told you everything if I thought you would believe me."

"I would have believed anything you told me. You're my best friend," I say. "No matter what."

"All right. I'll tell you everything." He looks away, takes a breath. "I lied to you."

I brace myself, wondering which thing he said was a lie. "I'm a manly, godlike creature." Or "I stayed with you all night in the bathroom." Or maybe even "I don't want to break up with you." What? "About?"

"When I said I came back east to live closer to my dad because he wanted me back," he says, shrugging. "You know my dad and I have never been on the best of terms. Truth is, I had to leave."

"You had to?"

He exhales slowly. "It's crazy."

"Using the stars to control how people see you is crazy. But I believe you. Why did you have to leave?"

"How did you know about the Luminati?"

I'm relieved that he doesn't deny it this time. "Christian. The guy who works at the bakery. He told me. He's former Luminati."

"Is he the one that you . . ." He scratches his head. "I guess that's not important. I had to leave because I was in trouble."

"What kind of trouble?"

"The fevers. There were a lot of people in my school getting sick and my grandmother found out I was responsible for it. She warned me to stop but I couldn't. And then this girl—someone I didn't even know, from another school—died. I didn't have anything to do with it, but some Luminati did. Her mother wanted answers and some people came forward and then suddenly there was this media storm and everyone was talking about the Luminati. It turned into this big witch hunt. My grandmother told me and my mom that we needed to leave, to get as far away from the hysteria as possible. And so we did."

"Oh. I think that's why Christian came here, too. I think his girlfriend might have been the one who died. But he stopped," I say.

Wish sighs. "Good for him," he says, his voice bitter. "I wish I could, Gwen. I wish it every day. I hate being someone I'm not." He looks at the ground and rakes his hand through his hair. "I've tried to stop. I have. But I can't. I know it doesn't make any sense."

"Maybe you just need a little help," I suggest.

He sighs again. "I'd hoped that I could come back here and just be the old me. Really I did. I even postponed the flight because I was thinking that would allow more time for it to wear off. But then Terra emailed me, saying that all the girls in school had seen my pictures on Facebook and thought I was so hot, and they couldn't wait to see me. And I knew I was in trouble. I know it sounds stupid and superficial but I was afraid I'd disappoint everyone if I showed up looking like my old self. It took everything for me to get on that plane and come here. I almost didn't."

"But what is so bad about who you really are?"

He shakes his head. "Nothing. Everything. Maybe it would have been okay if I had come here looking like a wallflower, if I had blended."

"You were never a wallflower. Everyone always liked you."

"But because of the pictures, everyone expected a rock star. And now everyone thinks that's what I am. I don't want to see the looks on their faces when they realize I'm just . . . me."

"Actually, I don't really like the rock star."

He lets out a short laugh. "I noticed that. I think that's the only thing that's kept me sane." Then he turns to me, a miserable look in his eyes. Even when he was the old Wish, I've never seen him look so uncertain about himself. "But I don't think you will like what I really am. And you know, I don't care about anyone else. I just don't want to lose you."

"You're crazy," I whisper, tears flooding my eyes. "You're an idiot. Do you really think I care how you look?"

He shrugs. "Everybody else seems to."

"I'm not them." I put a hand on his arm, but he's so warm it shocks me. I quickly pull my fingers away.

His frown deepens. "Sorry. We take on the properties of the stars. We glow. We radiate heat. My body temperature is over one hundred and ten degrees. And we pass that on to everyone around us. I guarantee you have a fever right now, too. A little one. But some people get it worse, are affected more."

"You mean Evie?"

He nods. "I didn't mean to hurt them. Destiny and Evie are skinny little things, so maybe that's why."

So I guess there's one positive thing about the junk in my trunk. I think about what Evie said to me, about Erica and Wish at the party. She made it up. She was jealous of me, however unbelievable that may sound. I smile and sing-song, "Or maybe it's because they have huge crushes on you."

He shrugs. "Maybe. But big deal. They have crushes on someone who isn't real."

I struggle for a bit, trying to think of a way to convince him that everything lovable about him has nothing to do with his packaging. "Um. Hello? Don't be dense. Don't you realize how easy it is to fall in love with you? Your personality, your sweetness, your sense of humor . . ."

He studies me, as if to say, "Are you serious?" "I could say the same thing to you."

I feel my cheeks reddening, but I don't think it's just from the fever. "Oh, please."

"It's true."

"Oh." Once I've remembered to breathe again, I say, "So what are you going to do now?"

He shakes his head sadly. "I want to stop, of course. I don't know how, though. I am so sorry, Gwen. I screwed everything up. Everything. Because of my stupidity, I almost lost you. And you're the only thing that matters to me."

I swallow. I think about pressing the nurse's button, because if it's possible for someone to die of happiness, I'm almost there. "Really?"

"No, I'm lying." His face is completely serious. Then he laughs. "Come on."

"Where is your tattoo?" I ask.

"I'll show you," he says, and I hold my breath, wondering what possibly throbbing body part he might expose to me. But he stretches the neck of his T-shirt and there it is, in a nice, respectable place on his shoulder blade.

I scoot to the edge of the bed to look at it. It's only the size of a dime and it looks like a slightly elaborate asterisk. "Oh. I can't believe that little mark has so much power."

"Tell me about it. I wish I could get rid of it. But people have tried to have them removed and I guess it doesn't work."

"I know. You could tattoo over it. It makes it less powerful." He gives me a questioning look. "Christian told me."

"Oh." He looks at the mark and then starts to scratch it.

"Gah. It itches like crazy. And even if I tattoo over it, it will still have power over me. I'm screwed."

"No, you're not. I'll help you. We can do it together. Okay?"

He looks at me doubtfully. "We just went over this. Nothing can help me."

"You are not screwed. You just need to know that you can do this without the stars. Because you have something better than them. Me."

I put on my most determined face. I have no idea where I mustered the confidence for that, but it works, because he laughs, and not in a "you've got to be kidding" way, but in a way that says he believes that maybe I can help. "All right. How do you expect to help me?"

"Remember what you said in your email? About how you wanted to . . ."

He doesn't even take the time to think it over, as if it was at the top of his mind, all this time. "Kiss you?"

"Yeah. Do you still want to?"

He nods. "Very much. Every day."

"Oh." I'm full-force blushing now. "Why didn't you, then?"

"You didn't seem interested."

"Oh, no, I am. Just, I've never . . ." Am I really going to admit to this? I must have been hit on the head harder than I thought.

He puts a finger on my lips. "It's okay." I never imagined that my first kiss would take place on a hospital bed, under horrid fluorescent lighting, surrounded by beeping machines and bedpans. I always imagined stars, but screw that; I don't like the stars very much right now. I also thought candlelight, classical music, soft tropical breezes would come into play. I also imagined that I would have just returned from a victorious whirlwind trip to *The Dr. Oz Show*, where I'd told an entire audience of jealous housewives how I'd managed to lose a hundred pounds.

I thought that I would be wearing something other than a gown with pink bunnies on it, open down the back. That I would have makeup on, and that my hair would smell of something other than seaweed and dead fish. That I would have, at the very least, brushed my teeth.

Oh, no, I think as he moves closer. No no no. "Wait, I need to, like . . . I just woke up. I'm disgusting. Do you have any toothpaste?"

He straightens, pretends to check his pockets. "Um. Not on me."

"Oh." The bathroom seems like miles away, but this is more important than a concussion or whatever is wrong with my head. This is an emergency. "Well, I can just—"

Then he grabs my hands in his own warm ones and laughs. "You're perfect." He puts a hand through my hair, starting at the crown and reaching to the back of my head, then gently pulls me to him, his soft lips meeting mine. I feel the heat of his skin against my clammy body, and maybe it's enough to make steam, because everything blurs so much that I squeeze my eyes closed and just concentrate on the taste of him. It's something even my mother's best baked creation could never come close to. "See? You're so sweet. Salty, actually," he whispers.

"You're not so bad yourself." I can barely get out the words, since every part of me is trembling.

"You know," he murmurs into my neck, "I think you may have just discovered the cure."

And it only takes a minute before I am really, really glad we're not *just* best friends.

38

MELINDA'S CORAL SUITE has so much lace and macramé that it makes a young person age a few years just looking at it. But it's home, for now. Amazingly, the top floor of her hotel got practically no damage, so she offered my mom, Evie, and me the best room. It's cramped for three people, but it's better than our other two options: the street or the Whitecap Room, in the attic. That's Christian's room. One morning, a week after the storm, I creep up there, and it's stifling. Plus the ceiling is only six feet high, so it feels like living in a box.

I knock on the door and a voice calls, "Come in." When I open it, someone is flopped on his stomach on the bed. Not Christian, though. Someone else.

"Um, I was looking for . . ."

He turns over. And I recognize the face. It *is* Christian.

The tattoos are still there, but the dreads are gone. Instead, he has a buzz cut and looks like he's about to join the navy. He closes a dusty old book, probably another coma-inducing literary masterpiece, and smiles a little. "Tell your boyfriend thanks for me."

"What?" I'm too busy taking in his new look to hear him. We haven't seen much of each other in the past week, but that's because I've had so much going on. Recovering from my concussion. Sorting through the remains of the bakery. Spending nearly every other free moment with Wish, helping to cure him of his addiction to perfection. Obviously a lot of lip balm has been involved.

"I much prefer this weather." Christian runs his hands through his bristly hair. "You like it? I'm trying something new. The clean-cut thing."

"Oh. It's nice." I can see his eyes completely now, and they're big and blue and totally intense. In fact, they're so intense I find myself blank, trying to remember why I came up here. Oh, right. Melinda. "Melinda wants you downstairs. She needs help moving something. Something big. Like a sofa or something."

"Ah. She needs the brawny man-help," he says in a low, gruff voice. I expect him to begin flexing his muscles. Instead, he just gets to his feet and, ducking under the low ceiling, says, "Cool, thanks." Then he smiles, and there's a little shyness in the way he fidgets in front of me. "You look nice."

I glance down. I was able to salvage some clothes from Melinda's bag, so I'm wearing a red blouse instead of the ratty gym shorts and tee I've been wearing all week, while we were trying to sort through the mess in the bakery. Today's the first day back to school, so I felt the need to take a little care with my appearance. "Thanks."

He shrugs. "I guess things are finally working out for you and your boyfriend?"

"Yes, they are, thank you very much," I say. I could say that it's completely thanks to him, which it is, but I'm afraid he'll get a big head.

I wait for the inevitable sarcastic remark, which comes a second later. He digs his hands into his pockets and says, "Too bad."

I scowl at him.

"No, I mean . . ." He grins sheepishly. "We could have gone out or something. If I'd been the one to get you out, instead of that boyfriend of yours."

I nearly gag on my tongue. Is he serious? "What?"

He takes a step toward the staircase and says, "I'm glad you're okay now. I was worried about you."

"Oh, well, th-th-thanks," I stammer.

He's staring at me like I have something in my teeth. "Wh-wh-what? You don't believe me?"

"Honestly, no. I thought . . . I thought you hated me, really."

He winks. "Maybe that's just what I wanted you to think."

"Oh, right. You *are* a scumbling screwfinger," I groan, but I can't help smiling.

He grins. "Have fun at school, beautiful," he says, leaving me alone to listen to the creaking of the hardwood floors under his feet.

Beautiful. I repeat the word to myself once, twice, three times. This time, though, I don't turn around to see what supermodel is standing behind me. I may even believe that he's right, that that's a perfect way to describe me, and has been all along.

I follow him down the stairs and go back to the Coral Suite, where Evie is standing by the window and munching on a handful of Cheerios. "I miss sticky buns so so so so much," she groans, looking at the tiny little O's in her hand with disdain.

"Tell me about it." I thought I'd eaten enough white cream donuts to last me a lifetime, but it wasn't even close.

She turns and studies me. "You've lost weight."

"Really?" I ask, looking down at my body. Maybe it's just the clothes. Or that ever since Evie got home from the hospital, she's been super-nice to me. It's her way of repaying me for the lie she told me about Wish and Erica, without having to come straight out and say "I'm sorry." I can't say I've paid much attention to my body recently; I just haven't had the time. I know that not having the bakery around has made getting morning, afternoon, and evening pick-me-ups difficult, but I haven't wanted them much. I've been busy with other things. I realize I haven't even thought about weighing myself in days, which must be a new record for me.

She sighs and pushes a lace curtain back into place. Her head hangs. "My ride is here. Oh, joy."

"Bus?" I ask.

She nods and swallows as if she has a sore throat, then fixes her dark sunglasses over her eyes.

"Wish'll give you a ride."

She nearly jumps into my arms. "Really?"

"Duh. Of course."

"Yes!" She shouts, pumping her fist. She runs downstairs to tell the bus driver to begone and returns a few minutes later. "Thanks, Dough."

. "No prob," I say.

"Rick is a turd," she says under her breath.

"I could have told you that. In fact, I think . . . I seem to remember that I did," I say.

"Whatever," she mutters, shoving the entire handful of O's into her mouth.

I shrug. "Well, he does have a really nice car. Who could blame you? I was kind of jealous myself."

She swallows and gives me an "are you kidding?" look. "Of me? You are so weird, Dough."

I hear a horn beeping outside. Wish. When we run out to his truck in the early-morning chill, he's there, in his rumpled white T-shirt and sunglasses, chewing on his bottom lip and looking nervous. Supposedly, he's different. I know that because when we go out together, he doesn't turn heads like he used to. When we went to Friday's, the waitress didn't give him doe eyes and there was no drool glistening in the corner of her mouth. And his cell phone doesn't ring every two seconds, like it used to. But to me, he looks perfect. He hasn't changed a bit. If anything, he's better than before. Can that be possible?

He pulls the front seat forward for Evie, and she's about to climb into the back when she stops abruptly and stares at him, as if she doesn't quite believe it's him. She's been too "busy" to help with the cleaning, so she hasn't seen him in a while. "Wish?"

"It's me," he says, looking a little embarrassed.

"What happened to you?" she asks, wrinkling her nose. "Were you sick, too?"

"Um. Yeah. I guess," he answers, looking at me and shrugging.

We all climb in. "Everything will be fine," I say to him as he throws the truck into gear so roughly that the transmission squeals.

"Oh. I know," he says. "I was just thinking."

"Of what?"

"Whether I'd rather go to school today or eat a razor blade. I think school wins. Just by a hair." He looks at me. "You?"

"Is it a safety razor blade?"

"No. Full razory goodness."

"Yeah. You're right. School."

He thinks for a moment as we coast over the bridge. This time, the seagulls on the streetlights don't seem to be paying us much attention. "Would you rather listen to Erica spout on about how awesome she is or lick the inside of a toilet bowl?"

"Um . . ." We look at each other for a moment. At the same time, we both nod and say, "Toilet bowl."

Then we can't stop laughing. Evie groans at us in the backseat and looks like she wishes she'd opted for the bus. "You two so belong together," she mumbles, sinking in her seat and burying her face in her knobby knees.

We ignore her. We keep playing. The game goes on and on until the inside of the truck disappears, and once again we're in the back of the bakery, with a stack of board games and a long, lazy summer day stretching ahead of us. It's just me and Wish. Me and my best friend.

He fidgets with the radio buttons, unable to keep still, when we pull up to the school. I put my hand on his. It's totally cool now, and mine feels hot against it. When we get out of the truck, Evie jogs ahead, pretending not to know us. Wish takes a big breath and looks at me. "Are you ready?"

I shrug. "For school? Never."

He shakes his head, and for a moment I think he might just make a run for the woods and disappear. Instead, he stretches his arms out at his sides, as far as he can reach. "For Gone with the Wind."

I laugh, spreading my arms like wings. "Oh, yeah. Always ready for that."

"Then let's go."

We start across the street, and he grabs my hand. Lacing our fingers together, we race breathlessly toward the school, on the wind, like two crazy people, two kindred spirits, laughing all the way.

CYN BALOG is addicted to white cream donuts and once gained fifteen pounds over the summer working at a bakery. She lives in Pennsylvania with her husband and daughters. She is also the author of the young adult novels *Fairy Tale* and *Sleepless*. Visit her online at cynbalog.com.